Mother McCrea, what a smile!

Women probably melted in puddles at his feet. Certain she would never see Flynn again, Mary Kate lowered her gaze, sweeping it over his lean body one last time, storing in her memory every perfect detail.

Flynn felt that heated appraisal clear to his toes. He saw the unexpected gleam in her eye when she once more raised her gaze to meet his. His control snapped. Though his brain screamed *Don't do it*, he reached for her, smothering her protest with a hungry kiss. For a heartbeat she was his, and then she twisted free.

She touched her gloved fingertips to her lips. "You *kissed* me," Mary Kate accused with obvious disbelief.

"Yes," Flynn agreed with a dazed nod.

Dear Reader,

Welcome to Silhouette—experience the magic of the wonderful world where two people fall in love. Meet heroines that will make you cheer for their happiness, and heroes (be they the boy next door or a handsome, mysterious stranger) who will win your heart. Silhouette Romance reflects the magic of love—sweeping you away with books that will make you laugh and cry, heartwarming, poignant stories that will move you time and time again.

In the coming months we're publishing romances by many of your all-time favorites, such as Diana Palmer, Brittany Young, Sondra Stanford and Annette Broadrick. Your response to these authors and our other Silhouette Romance authors has served as a touchstone for us, and we're pleased to bring you more books with Silhouette's distinctive medley of charm, wit and—above all—*romance*.

I hope you enjoy this book and the many stories to come. Experience the magic!

Sincerely,

Tara Hughes
Senior Editor
Silhouette Books

LINDA VARNER

The Luck of the Irish

Silhouette *Romance*

Published by Silhouette Books New York

America's Publisher of Contemporary Romance

To my daddy, Joe Varner,
with thanks for sharing with me
his love of a good book and those wonderful
Donald Lam/Bertha Cool mysteries

And to Gina Wilkins
with thanks for bailing me out
time and time again

SILHOUETTE BOOKS
300 E. 42nd St., New York, N.Y. 10017

Copyright © 1989 by Linda Varner Palmer

ISBN: 0-373-08665-2

First Silhouette Books printing August 1989

Printed in the U.S.A.

Books by Linda Varner

Silhouette Romance

Heart of the Matter #625
Heart Rustler #644
The Luck of the Irish #665

LINDA VARNER

has always had a vivid imagination. For that reason, while most people counted sheep to get to sleep, she made up romances. The search for a happy ending sometimes took more than one night, and when one story grew to mammoth proportions, Linda decided to write it down. The result was her first romance novel.

Happily married to her junior high school sweetheart, the mother of two, and a full-time secretary, Linda still finds that the best time to plot her latest project is late at night when the house is quiet and she can create without interruption. Linda lives in Conway, Arkansas, where she was raised, and believes the support of her family, friends and writers' group made her dream of being published come true.

Chapter One

So this is where your precious Jessie works," Flynn Rafferty commented as he seated himself across the table from his longtime buddy, Brandon "Tex" Charleston. His dark eyes swept the pub, taking in every detail of the paneled walls, the polished wooden floor, and the glassware sparkling on a shelf behind the mahogany bar. Unconsciously he nodded his approval, realizing he could well have been in Ireland, home of his ancestors, instead of in this picturesque bar in Boulder, Colorado.

"This is it," the blonde replied, sweeping his arm to include the smoke-hazed room. "Or should I say, 'This *was* it.' When she gets off tonight, I'm taking her away from O'Malley's Pub for good." He took off his cowboy hat and set it on the table.

Flynn shook his head and gave his Southern friend a worried frown. "Assuming she agrees to this crazy elopement, that is. I can't believe she'd want to take on the mindboggling task of being wife to one over-the-hill and overworked loan officer. I can't even believe you asked her in the first place. Do you realize it was just six weeks ago that we toasted perpetual bachelorhood? What the hell happened?''

Tex shrugged and grinned. "What can I say? She came, she saw, she conquered. One look at those baby blues and I didn't have a prayer."

Flynn snorted at that. "It's not too late to back out," he suggested softly, glancing toward the bar just in time to see a costumed waitress come from the back through a swinging door. The sudden gleam in his friend's eye told Flynn that the pretty brunette was probably Jessica. Busy with a tray of clean glasses, she hadn't spotted the pair yet. "There's still time to change your mind. This wedding is supposed to be next month, and she isn't expecting you—doesn't even know you're here."

Tex grinned the half-witted grin of a man in love and stood up, waving to catch Jessica's eye. She did a double take and flashed him a brilliant smile. Tex dropped back into his chair. He gave a helpless shrug. "Thanks for the offer, but I'm not budging."

Flynn groaned his disgust. How could a die-hard bachelor like Tex Charleston, a man who for years had dodged marriage-minded females with a skill that rivaled Flynn's own, have gotten into such a state? Flynn glanced once more toward the bar, reluctantly admiring Jessica's glowing face. She was clearly as besotted as Tex. Something akin to envy tugged briefly at his heart before he ruthlessly suppressed it. He must be getting soft in the head himself, he decided. Tex was about to make a serious mistake, and it was up to Flynn to talk him out of it.

"Think of what you're getting into," he cautioned. "Think of the responsibility...."

"The fun," countered Tex.

"The mortgage."

"The square meals."

"The fights," Flynn warned.

"Making up."

"The lost weekends mowing lawns, doing laundry, buying groceries."

Tex grinned at his frustrated friend. "Sweet, sweet Jessie in my bed every night."

Flynn threw up his hands in exasperation. "For God's sake, have you lost your mind?"

Tex merely laughed.

In desperation, Flynn tried another tack. "What about fatherhood, man? Are you ready for diapers, midnight feedings, the PTA?"

Tex's smile faded. He gave his lady love a long, thoughtful look and then nodded slowly. "Yeah. Yeah, I am. And it's time you gave wedded bliss some serious consideration yourself. You're thirty-three years old. You can't play the field forever. One of these days you're going to take a look around, old buddy, and realize there's more to life than a Jeep, a condo, and a different date every Saturday night."

Flynn didn't even grace that foolishness with a reply, instead sinking back in his chair. Clearly Tex was too far gone to save. Flynn would have to carry on alone—the last of the confirmed bachelors. "How could you let a thing like this happen?"

Tex shrugged. "It was love at first sight."

"Love at first sight?" Flynn scoffed. "Give me a break."

Tex shook a finger at him, scolding, "Don't laugh, old friend. It could happen to you, too."

"No, it couldn't, and I'll tell you why," Flynn told him solemnly. "I never *ever* drop my guard. I don't even begin a relationship on any level unless I've got a handle on it. Then, if the situation looks promising, if things get hot—" he grinned "—I find out everything there is to know about the female in question, from her shoe size to her mother's maiden name, before I proceed. In other words, *I stay in control*. That's where you went wrong, my friend. You lost control.''

A riotous mass of silky russet curls appeared from no-where, momentarily blocking his view of same foolish friend. Flynn caught his breath in surprise, inadvertently inhaling the scent of the waitress now setting frosty goblets of ice water on the green linen tablecloth in front of him. She smelled of sunshine—a fresh, sexy smell that made his eyes widen and his heart thud. His gaze traveled up over her slender arm and neck to rest on her face—oval-shaped, flushed and lightly freckled. Huge emerald eyes—laughing eyes—caught the glow of the candles set about the room, bewitching him with their sparkle. Flynn almost forgot how to breathe.

She smiled. ''Hi, guys. I'll be your waitress tonight. Would you like to see a menu?''

Oblivious to all but the shapely beauty at his side, Flynn got slowly to his feet, straightening to his full height and topping her by a good seven or eight inches. Mesmerized, he extended his right hand. ''Flynn Rafferty. And you're...?''

She blinked, clearly startled by the unexpected introduc-tion, but gave him her hand. ''Uh, Mary Kate O'Connor.''

''Ahh,'' he murmured with a slow nod, covering that dainty hand with his other one. ''That explains the mis-chief in those eyes. You're Irish.''

''Yes,'' she replied, prying her peach-tipped fingers out of his death grip and then swiping them down the frilly white apron that gave her uniform its Gaelic air.

''So am I,'' he told her. ''And that, Mary Kate, me dar-lin', doubles the mischief we're going to make together.'' Flynn flicked an absent glance at Tex, who suddenly went into a fit of coughing.

''Why, you—!'' She caught herself in time, glancing quickly toward a large man standing at the cash register just a few feet away. Then she turned, and without another word, fled.

Flynn watched her until she disappeared through the swing doors that undoubtedly led to the kitchen. Gradually he became aware of the real world—the hum of dozens of conversations, the muted strains of a rock ballad, the hearty laughter of his old friend. Flynn frowned in confusion, shaking his head as though that might clear his muddled brain.

"What's so damn funny?" he demanded, sitting down.

"You are," Tex retorted, laughing again. He leaned forward until his nose was inches from Flynn's. "Didn't you just hit on a total stranger? And with an Irish brogue, no less."

"Don't be ridiculous," Flynn retorted. Then he frowned, replaying the last few, oddly hazy moments of his life. He realized abruptly that Tex had, indeed, witnessed such a thing; and he flushed. "Not a total stranger," he qualified lamely. "I knew her name."

Tex leaned back, slapping his flattened palm to his forehead. *"Da-amn,"* he drawled, giving the expletive two syllables. "That suave—" he pronounced it *swave* "—introduction slipped my mind."

"Will you just shut up?" Flynn snapped, thoroughly flustered by his actions moments ago.

"Shut up?" Tex echoed in disbelief. "Did the man who's been harassing me for hours about losing control actually ask me to shut up?" He laughed maliciously. "Fat chance, pardner."

The dark-haired Irishman leaned forward, his eyes narrowed in annoyance. "I had a momentary lapse, okay? It happens to the best of us."

"And you're going to find that poor young woman and apologize?" Tex teased, undaunted by his ire.

"Of course I am," Flynn told him, silently adding, *when my hands quit shaking.* "I don't know what happened just then, but the important thing is that I'm in control again now, and that's more than I can say for you."

Tex merely grinned, his thoughtful blue gaze following his friend's troubled brown one across the bar to a still-swinging door.

"Mary Kate!" Jessica Wilson exclaimed excitedly, clutching her friend's arm. "You'll never believe who's out front!"

Mary Kate peeked out one of the narrow rectangular windows in the door through which she'd escaped seconds before. She drew a shaky breath. "A crazy man?"

"Of course not," Jessica responded with a frown. "It's Tex!"

"Tex?" Mary Kate murmured absently, her eyes glued to the handsome stranger who'd just annihilated her pub-famous cool with his prediction. She barely registered the young woman's news.

"Yes. Tex," Jessica repeated. She gave Mary Kate a little shake. "Tex Charleston, my fiancé. At table seven. That's your table tonight. Do you mind switching with me? You can have table three."

"No problem," Mary Kate agreed, suddenly remembering just who Tex was—the young man with whom Jessica had fallen in love when she went to a Denver finance company to apply for a student loan a few weeks ago. Then Mary Kate froze, turning to her friend in horror. "Did you say table seven?"

Jessica nodded eagerly.

Mary Kate gulped and ventured, "Tall, dark-haired guy with a mustache?"

Bubbly laughter greeted her horrified question. "No, no. He's blond. Blue eyes, dimples . . ."

Whew! "I get the picture," Mary Kate assured her dreamy-eyed friend with relief. Glad to find that the stranger who'd left her breathless and flustered moments ago was not her co-worker's boyfriend, Mary Kate looked out the window again. She let her eyes drink in every detail of the flashing brown eyes, curly dark hair and full mustache of her nemesis. His gray three-piece suit showed off his muscular build to perfection—wide shoulders, broad chest. What a specimen!

Too bad he's loco, she thought regretfully. Loco? Because he'd spouted some blarney about their making mischief together? Hadn't more than one male customer with too many beers under his belt done the same since she'd started working here two months ago? Of course they had, and that, she suddenly realized, was exactly what bothered her about Flynn Rafferty. The possessive gleam in his mahogany eyes had been stone sober. He wasn't drunk, just incredibly conceited. "Who's that guy at the table with Tex?" she asked as casually as possible.

Jessica stepped to the other door and peered out. "I don't know for sure, but I'll bet it's Flynn Rafferty, his best friend." She turned to Mary Kate and grinned, not fooled for a minute. "Easy on the eyes, isn't he?"

Mary Kate blushed at Jessica's intuitive question. "Yes, and speaking of eyes, hadn't you better keep yours on your cowboy, who's not half bad himself?"

"Some cowboy," Jessica replied with a giggle. "In spite of that Stetson he sports, I'll bet that sweetheart of mine has never even been on a horse." She smoothed down her apron and skirt, and then fluffed her dark hair. "Do I look all right?"

"You look fantastic," Mary Kate assured her.

Jessica peeked out the window again. "I can't believe he risked his neck to drive from Denver tonight. He doesn't have a four-wheel drive like I do, and there's a blizzard out there. I was afraid I wouldn't get to see him again until the wedding.''

''Where there's a will, there's a way,'' her red-haired friend reminded her, giving her a gentle push toward the door. Grinning, Jessica disappeared through it. Mary Kate watched her walk to the table. The handsome blonde leaped to his feet immediately, greeting Jessica with a hug and kiss that told Mary Kate it would take more than a snowstorm to keep him from her friend of two months. Mary Kate couldn't help but smile at the sight, letting her gaze drift over to the other occupant of the table. She noted that Flynn wasn't smiling, and she wondered if he had his doubts about this engagement, too. After all, Jessica and Tex were practically strangers.

''O'Connor!''

The pub manager's unexpected growl burst into Mary Kate's distraction and she jumped guiltily, realizing her boss was now in the kitchen, watching her with ill-concealed impatience. Since she'd just wasted a good ten minutes and on a Friday night, she snatched up a tray of clean glasses and backed out the doors, determined to get to work and stay well clear of that dark-eyed Irishman.

Four and three-quarters hours later found Flynn sitting alone at the same table in the almost deserted pub, patiently waiting for closing time. Not surprisingly, Jessica had agreed to Tex's proposal, and Flynn now realized that in another few minutes the pair would drive off into the proverbial sunset, bringing to a halt years of bachelor antics. It was a shame—a damned shame. Oh, it wasn't that Flynn didn't like Jessica. He did—a lot more than he'd planned to, in fact. And it wasn't that he blamed Tex. He didn't—not really. He just couldn't understand how his friend could be so positive that Jessica was the woman for him. And he sure was going to miss the evenings filled with his pal's outrageous tall tales.

At that moment Tex returned to the table, plopping down in the chair beside him. "Flynn," he said, his face troubled. "We've hit a snag."

"What's wrong?" Flynn asked. "Can't find a JP willing to perform a midnight ceremony?" He could think of nothing else that might stop this wedding. Tex and Jessica had gotten the marriage license days ago.

"No, I've got that part all worked out—or did have. Jessica just remembered she promised to give a friend who's having car trouble a ride home. We'll have to drop her off on our way out—unless you're willing to help...?"

Flynn shook his head at Tex's hopeful expression. "Relax. I'll do the honors, but I still think this whole elopement is a big mistake."

Tex ignored that. A wide smile split his face. "Thanks, buddy," he gushed, slapping Flynn on the back. "I owe you." He swiveled in the chair, giving a thumbs-up sign to Jessica, who beamed her relief from across the room.

Flynn glanced past her, unerringly locating Mary Kate O'Connor, who had her back to him. He knew now would be a good time to get up and make his apologies, but he delayed yet again, convincing himself she was too busy clearing a table in a far corner of the pub. Flynn couldn't drag his gaze away from her, and that bothered him as much as his unforgivable behavior earlier. He decided Mary Kate must be one of the wee folk, a fairy who'd cast a spell on him. Then he grinned at his fanciful musings.

A second later his grin vanished. Her movements had raised her short skirt even higher at the back, affording a tantalizing glimpse of shapely thighs and a lacy, beribboned garter. Flynn gulped audibly and groped for the pack of cigarettes lying on the table near Tex, actually lighting one before he remembered he'd quit six months ago. Snorting his disgust, he stubbed it out and reached for his drink instead.

Tex's gaze followed Flynn's across the room. When the blonde spotted the reason for his friend's distraction, he laughed malevolently, a now-familiar sound that had begun to grate on Flynn's nerves. Tex leaned toward him just as he sipped the liquid, asking, "Sure you're up to driving her home?"

Flynn choked and grabbed for a napkin, struggling to swallow the fizzing cola. "*She* needs the ride?" he blurted between coughs.

Tex grinned mischievously. "Yep."

"Damn."

"Is something wrong?" Tex asked with exaggerated bewilderment.

"No," Flynn lied, his eyes never leaving the redheaded, green-eyed slip of a lass who made his heart thunder and his wits take a leave of absence.

"I know she kind of got to you, at first," Tex went on as if he hadn't spoken. "But you still need to apologize, and you *did* say you were in control again...."

"I am," Flynn assured him with a quick glance at his watch: eleven fifty-six. In four minutes the pub would close, and shortly after, he would be alone in his Jeep with a sorceress. What a thought. He drew a shuddering breath. Then he cast an accusing look toward his friend. "Does she really need a ride, or is this something you cooked up?"

"She needs a ride," Tex assured him. When Flynn didn't respond, he added, "If I lie, I die. Something bigger than me has brought you two together tonight. It's fate or maybe that Irish luck of yours."

"Irish luck is good, not bad," Flynn told him.

"You call a chance with a looker like her *bad* luck?" Tex sputtered in disbelief. Clearly he doubted his old friend's sanity.

Flynn glanced back at Mary Kate, now deep in conversation with Jessica. He saw her look his way and shake her head firmly. He winced. So she wasn't any more thrilled about the arrangement than he was, and probably for a different reason altogether. No doubt she thought he was some kind of geek. That wasn't surprising, considering he'd actually come on to her—and using that corny brogue he'd picked up from his granddad. He couldn't believe he'd done such a thing, and his considerable male pride couldn't tolerate the opinion of him she undoubtedly harbored as a result.

"No," he said firmly, as the fighting Irish in him reasserted itself. Suddenly he welcomed this opportunity to set things straight. "I call that sensational." He leaned back slightly, crossing his arms over his chest and issuing across the pub a silent challenge he hoped the fighting Irish in *her* couldn't ignore. Mary Kate saw it, stiffened, and grabbed Jessica's arm, dragging the brunette into the kitchen. Three minutes later, Jessica burst through the swinging doors again—alone and obviously agitated.

"Mary Kate says 'No thanks,'" she blurted when she reached the table. "She's going to bum a ride home with one of the bartenders." Jessica grasped Tex's arm. "You've got to do something. Every one of those turkeys has had at least two beers, and the roads are treacherous tonight."

Flynn took one look at Tex's woebegone expression and got to his feet. Though his friend deserved a little hell for all the ribbing he'd dished out this night, Flynn didn't have the heart to give it to him. Tex had spent a good hour on the phone, working out every last detail of this wedding, and a justice of the peace now waited out there somewhere. Far be it for Flynn to delay the honeymoon a moment longer than necessary. And besides, at the least, he owed Mary Kate O'Connor a ride home. "You two hit the road. I'll see Ms. O'Connor home."

"I don't know," Jessica replied, a doubtful look on her face. "She was pretty adamant, and not in a very good mood." She gave her fiancé an apologetic smile. "She thinks you and I are making a big mistake."

Tex exchanged a silent look with Flynn, who graciously didn't voice his support of Mary Kate's opinion. Instead Flynn said, "She'll come around. Don't worry about a thing."

Smiling his relief, Tex stood and extended a hand, which Flynn took. "Good luck, pal, and thanks—for everything."

"You're the one who's gonna need the luck," Flynn muttered softly.

Tex ignored that. "I'll be in touch," he promised before he put on his hat and ushered his beloved through the blend of customers and employees now leaving the bar. "And I'll see you at the office Monday morning."

"Make that Wednesday," Flynn impulsively informed his employee and best friend. "My gift to the bride."

Beaming their thanks, the pair donned their winter wraps in the foyer and disappeared out the door. Flynn stood staring after the two of them for a moment, his thoughts on weddings, honeymoons and "happily-forever-after." Again a feeling suspiciously like envy surfaced, and though he tried to ignore it, he found he couldn't. He felt strangely discontented—no, downright glum. He found himself wondering if there could possibly be a grain of truth in Tex's warning that someday the things he held dear might not be enough to make him happy. He thought of his life-style and tried to picture himself at forty, or fifty, or even sixty years old. He frowned, not pleased with what he envisioned.

"Damn that Tex," he muttered. Suddenly jostled, he stepped absently aside, letting two costumed waitresses slip past him on their way out. He glanced at his watch, noting that it was ten minutes past midnight. Determinedly he turned to go look for Mary Kate, only to collide with someone.

"Excuse me," he said automatically, catching that someone's arms to steady her. Green eyes—Mary Kate O'Connor's spellbinding green eyes—locked with his. Flynn looked away, deliberately holding his breath to keep from inhaling the magical scent of her. He stepped abruptly back.

"I—I was just coming to look for you," he stammered. Stammered? Flynn Rafferty? The skin under his too-tight collar got warm and the apology on the tip of his tongue stayed right where it was.

She didn't reply, merely raising an eyebrow in silent questioning.

"I promised Jessica and Tex that I'd drive you home," he said. "Are you ready to leave?"

Mary Kate eased free and took a step back, smiling coolly at him. "No thanks, Mr.—umm—"

"Rafferty," he supplied. "Flynn Rafferty."

"I remember now."

Flynn winced in embarrassment, her words bringing vividly to mind their first humiliating encounter. He reached up, unconsciously loosening his tie and the top button of his shirt so he could draw some air into his lungs. His neck and cheeks were more than warm now; they were hot, a sure sign he was blushing. Damn.

"It's very kind of you to offer, but I'd rather make other arrangements."

At that, she eased past him, joining the noisy throng of people clustered in the tiny foyer, most of whom were pulling on coats and boots before they faced the winter storm raging outside.

Now dead certain Mary Kate had slipped a love potion into his ice water, Flynn nonetheless followed her, halting at the jammed doorway when she forged a path to a phone booth tucked in a corner. Mary Kate thumbed through the thick directory, shut it and then picked up the receiver, inserting a coin into the slot. Curious, Flynn edged closer. She waited with obvious impatience, one hand over her free ear to block out the clamor in the crowded room.

"Would you please send a taxi to O'Malley's Bar on Twelfth Street?" he heard her ask. So she wasn't going to ride home with one of the tipsy bartenders, after all, Flynn realized. She was going to trust her life to some reckless cabbie with tread-bare tires instead. "What did you say? An hour? Are you serious?" she then blurted, obviously distressed. There was a long pause and then she murmured "Forget it" and hung up the phone. With a sigh of exasperation, she turned, blinking in surprise when she spotted Flynn, now only a couple of feet behind her.

"My offer still stands," he told her, determined to prove to himself that he could handle anything—even redheaded enchantresses.

"So does my answer," this particular one snapped. Her eyes left him, frantically searching the few people remaining in the foyer for a trustworthy face. Impulsively she reached out, grasping the arm of a man about to leave. "Bob, can you give me a lift home?"

"I'd love to, honey," the dark-haired male responded with a smile. "But I'm on my cycle. You'd freeze to death in that getup."

Mary Kate noted he wore an insulated jump suit and heavy boots. Cold-sensitive in the extreme and dead sure she wouldn't last ten minutes on a motorcycle, she released him, reluctantly nodding her agreement. Not for the first time, Mary Kate wondered what she, a native of the desert area of the Grand Canyon State, was doing living in a place as susceptible to having cold winters as Boulder, Colorado. But she knew why, and her reason was a good one—the best, in fact.

"Last chance."

Flynn Rafferty's husky voice broke into her thoughts. She saw he was shrugging into his coat, obviously about to leave. Her eyes roved his ruggedly handsome face, missing not one gorgeous detail of his chiseled jawline, sexy mustache and lopsided grin. She realized the goose bumps that suddenly danced up and down her arms had nothing at all to do with the weather.

"Look, I don't blame you for being leery of me," he said. "I acted like a jerk a while ago. I don't know what came over me." He cocked his head, his eyes beseeching her when he added, "Let me take you home—I owe you that, at least."

Dead certain she courted disaster, but equally certain she had no other option, Mary Kate relented. He seemed sincere. Surely she would be safe alone with him. "Oh, all right. Let me get my coat."

He nodded and stepped aside, letting her move toward the coatrack. She retrieved her red fox jacket—the one that matched her hair exactly—and slipped into it, buttoning it securely before she pulled on her woolen hat and gloves. Then she took a long scarf and wrapped it around her neck several times, her mind on the cold waiting just outside the door. When she'd finished that part of her ritual she glanced toward Flynn, who was waiting patiently with an amused look on his face.

"What's so funny?" she asked defensively.

"The top half of you should be toasty warm," he teased, his dark eyes twinkling. "But I've got serious doubts about the bottom half."

Mary Kate looked down at her legs, as good as bare from several inches above the knee on down, and realized the man had a point. "I'm not finished yet," she told him. She stepped out of her pumps and into a pair of fur-lined knee-high boots, zipping them from arch to top. Then she straightened. "See?"

"What I see is six or eight inches still exposed to the elements—a very nice six or eight inches, I might add."

Mary Kate's heart did a back flip. "I—I'll be okay," she stammered, as she crammed her shoes into the oversize handbag tucked under her arm. Stammered? Mary Kate O'Connor? She suddenly knew without a doubt that hitching a ride with this devastating Irishman was one giant mistake. She squared her shoulders, however, and mustering an enthusiasm she didn't really feel, said, "I'm ready now."

"Then let's get out of here."

His voice was suddenly cold and Mary Kate looked up at him in surprise, realizing he looked a little put-out. She didn't have time to wonder why before he caught her elbow, nudging her toward the exit. Outside, a blast of Arctic air stole the breath from Mary Kate's lungs, leaving her gasping.

"You okay?" Flynn asked, frowning worriedly at her when the pub door closed behind them, trapping the building's warmth and light inside.

With her body rigid, Mary Kate nodded, pulling her scarf up to cover her nose and mouth. She let him put his arms across her shoulders, guiding her down the snow-covered walkway to the almost-empty parking lot. She glanced overhead at the mercury vapor lights illuminating the area, noting with dismay that the swirling snow showed no signs of stopping in her lifetime.

"I should've warmed up the Jeep," Flynn apologized as he unlocked the door. It was frozen shut and opened with a crackling sound that made Mary Kate shiver. She climbed quickly inside, groaning her misery when her bare legs touched the freezing vinyl seat. Flynn stepped back, shutting the door. Seconds later he was behind the wheel. He inserted the key into the ignition, bringing the powerful engine to life. "When that little marker gets to right there," he told her, pointing to one of the gauges on the dashboard, "flip this switch."

Then he reached into the glove box for an ice scraper and got back out. Mary Kate shivered in the dark while he worked to clear the windshield. Anxiously she watched the marker, sighing her relief when it moved, indicating the engine was finally warm. She did as Flynn had instructed, reveling in the hot air that immediately blew out over her chilly knees.

In minutes, Flynn was in the Jeep again, putting the vehicle in gear and guiding it, lurching and jolting, over the snow-encrusted lot to the street. "Where to?" he asked her.

"Turn right here and then left at the light," she told him, her voice muffled by the scarf.

He glanced over at her and asked, "Warmer now?"

"I won't be warm until mid-April," she admitted. "I hate winter."

"That's too bad." He turned right and eased the Jeep onto the street. "I love it. That's one of the reasons I stay in Colorado instead of heading back south where I was born."

"So you're not a native, either?" she asked, settling back in the seat.

"I'm from Kentucky—Paducah, actually."

"I'm from Phoenix."

"No wonder you're cold," he commented. They approached the light, which was red, and halted. "You did say 'left'?"

"Yes, and then left again at the next light, about eight blocks from here. My apartment will be the third on the right."

Nodding his understanding, Flynn made the turn. She noted he drove skillfully down the perilous boulevard, always conscious of the other vehicles on the road. Luckily there weren't that many, no doubt due to the bad weather and the late hour. Mary Kate wished she were safe at home, up to her neck in hot water and bubbles, instead of in this noisy Jeep with its distressingly charming driver.

The fact that he was now acting like a perfectly normal and very desirable male only made matters worse. She was attracted to Flynn Rafferty, and the last thing she needed in her life right now was a man. Hadn't she just escaped four of them?

"I hope things went off without a hitch for Tex and Jessica," Mary Kate commented, to break the awkward silence that followed her directions.

Flynn turned at her thoughtless words. "If there's going to be a wedding night—and I'd bet my life that Tex was planning on one of those—you'd better hope there *was* a hitch."

"Uh, right," she responded hastily, blushing. She noted the set of his jaw and ventured, "You think they're crazy, too, don't you?"

He nodded firmly and another silence ensued. Lost in thought, Mary Kate didn't break this one. Several minutes later, Flynn turned down her street.

"One, two, three," he counted aloud as he passed the apartments lining either side. "This must be it." He turned into her drive, halting just behind her snow-blanketed car.

"It is," she told him. There was an awkward silence as they stared at each other, each fumbling for something clever to say. Mary Kate gave up first, muttering, "Thanks for coming to my rescue tonight. I'm getting a new battery for my car tomorrow. Hopefully that will end my hitchhiking career."

She pulled up the door handle, swinging her legs out and slipping to the ground. "Wait," Flynn exclaimed impulsively. "I'll walk you."

He slid across the seat and leaped out beside her. Together they stomped through the fluff, which measured midcalf and was hard to maneuver in. He clutched her arm, steadying her up the four steps to her lighted porch.

"Well, thanks again," she said, smiling self-consciously. She dug her house key out of her purse and unlocked the front door, all the while thinking what a nice man he really was—not at all the chauvinist she'd first thought him to be.

"Anytime," Flynn told her, relief washing over him. After that one wayward comment about her exposed anatomy, he'd done all right, actually getting her home in one piece and without making a total fool of himself. Inordinately pleased by that accomplishment, he relaxed slightly, lowering his guard just enough to return her smile.

Mary Kate's jaw dropped. Mother McCrea, what a smile! No wonder he used it so sparingly. Women probably melted in puddles at his feet every time he did. Certain she would never see Flynn again, Mary Kate lowered her gaze to sweep over his lean body one last time, storing in her memory every perfect detail.

Flynn felt that heated appraisal clear to his toes. He saw the unexpected gleam in her eye when she once more raised her gaze to meet his. His control snapped. In slow motion, he closed the distance between them, holding Mary Kate immobile with his eyes. Though his brain screamed *Don't do it!* he reached for her, smothering her protest with his hungry kiss. For a heartbeat she was his, and then she twisted free. She touched her gloved fingertips to her lips.

"You *kissed* me," Mary Kate accused with obvious disbelief.

"Yes," Flynn agreed with a dazed nod. Then he reached for her again.

Chapter Two

She was too quick for him this time, whirling and leaping for the safety of her apartment. In a flash she was inside, slamming the door, twisting the dead bolt with fingers that shook violently. She rested her forehead on the wooden barrier. Her heart raced, her breath came in pants. What a kiss! Unexpected, half a heartbeat long, and—devastating.

"Mary Kate? Are you all right?" Flynn's worried voice filtered through the wooden door almost immediately. She swallowed hard, refusing to answer him. "I know you can hear me. Tell me you're okay."

Okay? After a kiss like that? He had to be kidding.

"I'm sorry I did that. I don't know what's wrong with me tonight. I don't usually act this way." There was a long silence and then he pounded on the door. "Are you listening to me?"

"Go away," she replied.

"Not until you tell me you're all right."

"I'm all right. Now, go away." The silence following her words grew heavy. Curious, Mary Kate put her eye to the peephole. When she realized Flynn no longer stood on the porch, she hurried to the living room, sidestepping a large fern in a brass pot to reach the window. She pulled the drape aside just enough to peer out without being seen. Flynn was striding to the Jeep, his hands stuffed into the pockets of his overcoat.

Seconds later, the engine of that vehicle roared. He glanced toward the apartment building. Mary Kate immediately ducked behind the drape, and when she mustered the nerve to look out again, he was gone. She let the cloth fall back in place and turned, walking slowly back to the door to retrieve the purse she'd dropped in the lighted hallway moments before. Though she tried to suppress all thoughts of Flynn and his surprise kiss, she found she couldn't.

Instead she wondered what a longer, expected version of such a kiss would have been like. Mary Kate groaned aloud when she realized what direction her thoughts had taken. If her reaction to this brief but glorious contact were anything to go by, she was better off not finding out. Flynn was far too bold—if darned intriguing—and definitely not her type.

Or was he? Did she really know what kind of man appealed to her? Probably not, she admitted, since her romantic contact with the opposite sex had been rather haphazard, thus far. This was due as much to her full-time studies as to the four older brothers who insisted on monitoring her love life. But things were going to be somewhat different now. She was twenty-one and had a degree in a two-year business-college course. All her overprotective siblings were safe in Phoenix, over eight hundred miles away, and though her love life was still nonexistent, it was now by choice.

Mary Kate slipped out of her winter gear and put it in the closet, her thoughts on her home in Arizona. It was too bad she hadn't been this free three months ago when her mother and father left for Ireland to visit their aged parents. They'd invited her to go with them, had planned the trip as a graduation and turning-twenty-one present. But her paternal grandfather had unexpectedly died of a heart attack, and of necessity her parents had moved the trip forward several weeks so her dad could attend the funeral. Mary Kate had regretfully accepted the change in plans, knowing she couldn't abandon her classes when she was so close to completion. She wished she'd been able to see that spirited old grandfather of hers one last time. She loved him dearly, even though she'd actually met him only twice in her life.

Peeling off her "uniform" and sidestepping a potted palm tree, Mary Kate headed for the single bedroom and the hot bath she didn't really need anymore. She turned on the tap, acknowledging with some surprise that she was quite warm now, except for her perpetually chilly toes. She knew she owed Flynn thanks for this minor miracle—a realization that confirmed her suspicions that she didn't have any idea what kind of man appealed to her.

A product of a stable marriage and part of a large family, Mary Kate wanted those very things for herself—someday. But right now, fresh out of school and bursting with enthusiasm, she had places to go, people to see, and plans— all with capital *P*'s.

Monday she was going to go to the Denver finance company where Jessica had met Tex. She would see if she could sweet-talk that man into giving a loan to his new wife's friend, a woman with nothing but a head for business, a way with plants, and a dream. Then she would open her own flower shop, thumbing her nose with pleasure at all those smug bankers who'd taken one look at her loan application, laughed and handed it back to her.

Until that happened, she would spend her weekdays at her cousin's flower shop, The Daisy Patch, gaining valuable experience, and her nights at O'Malley's Pub, pocketing tips and resisting smooth-talking males. Mary Kate didn't have time for romance and didn't intend to let any man distract her from her one-track career course—even a tall, dark Irishman.

Monday morning and a new battery later, found Mary Kate mobile again and standing at a counter in the plush outer offices of Advantage Finance Company, pen and loan application in hand. She tried to concentrate on the paper in front of her, but found her thoughts ricocheting as they had ever since Flynn Rafferty burst into her life.

Name, the form asked for. She filled that in easily enough. Address. That wasn't hard, either. Phone number? No problem. Sex? *Might be fun,* she admitted, the memory of Flynn's kiss momentarily addling her logic. Mary Kate snorted in disgust, trying to force her thoughts back to the business at hand. Her future depended on this application. She could only hope this privately-owned loan company wouldn't have the same rigid guidelines that all the local banks seemed to have. Surely Tex wouldn't be able to resist the sight of a grown woman on her knees, begging.

Pushing those speculations aside, Mary Kate supplied the rest of the requested information with little difficulty, probably since she'd filled out several such forms lately. She signed her name on the bottom line of the last page with a flourish and glanced toward the receptionist's desk. The neatly dressed blonde who'd given her the papers minutes earlier was nowhere to be found, and Mary Kate let her gaze wander around the room.

She saw a closed door on her right and read the name painted on it: Brandon Charleston. Within minutes she would be in that very office, pleading her case. Her eyes swept the rest of the room, noting the thick carpet, elegant sofa and chairs and tasteful paintings, all of which bespoke a successful business. It looked as though Jessica's new husband had as good a job as she'd claimed, and that meant she would quit her job at O'Malley's to attend the University of Colorado full-time. Jessica had told Mary Kate that Tex supported her plans to get a degree in elementary education. Clearly he was one of those special men who wanted their spouses to be fulfilled—the kind of man Mary Kate hoped to find someday.

She tried to picture herself married, owning her own business, sharing her drive, dreams and future with a man who understood them. It wasn't easy, since her roots were very traditional. Her mother had abandoned a dream to be an interior decorator, deferring to her husband's demand that she devote her full energies to raising her children. She'd waited on her spouse and on their male offspring for years—still did, in fact. A very liberated Mary Kate watched her mother slave for the men in her life and had nightmares about getting caught in the same tender trap.

Mary Kate spotted a rather sad-looking shamrock sitting on one corner of the desk, and shook her head regretfully. She walked around the counter and picked it up, turning it this way and that to inspect the spindly, yellowed leaves.

"You poor thing," she sympathized aloud. Mary Kate talked to plants—always had—believing they needed TLC as much as the carbon dioxide naturally expelled from her lungs when she spoke. As a result, her house was filled with healthy, happy greenery.

"Pitiful, isn't it?"

Mary Kate smiled at the receptionist who had approached. "Yes, it is, but I can fix it for you."

"How?" the young woman asked skeptically.

"Got some scissors?"

Nodding, the slim blonde walked around to open a drawer in her desk. Wordlessly she handed Mary Kate a pair of scissors. Mary Kate took them and began to work on the plant, ruthlessly snipping off the overlong stems and sickly three-leafed clusters. Then she pulled out all the stems that had withered and were threatening the fragile root system.

"There. Now, don't overwater it—once a week is enough."

The receptionist stared in horror at the plant, which looked like it had just escaped from a barber with a hangover. "Oh, my God," she murmured. "That was my boss's plant."

"It'll be absolutely beautiful again in less than a week," Mary Kate assured her, bending down to add to the plant, "Won't you?" Then she impulsively murmured an old Gaelic blessing, one her grandfather had taught her years ago, the first time they'd met.

With obvious effort the young woman dragged her gaze away from the remains of the shamrock to ask, "Finished with your application?"

"Yes, I am. Do you think Tex Charleston will be able to see me today?"

"Oh, dear. I'm afraid he isn't here and won't be back in the office until Wednesday," the young woman told her. She smiled. "Tex got married this weekend."

"I know that, but I understood his fiancée to say they'd be back in town today," Mary Kate responded, frowning her disappointment. There must have been a last-minute change in plans. That was disastrous, especially since she'd been counting on the advantages of being Jessica's friend.

"He'll be back on Wednesday," the woman repeated firmly. She picked up the application. "Do you want to come back then, or would you like an appointment with the gentleman who's filling in for him?"

Mary Kate toyed with the idea of retrieving her request and returning on Wednesday. She abandoned that plan almost immediately, however, since she couldn't afford to sacrifice another day's pay. "I'd really like to see someone today, if possible. I took off work to be here."

The receptionist smiled her sympathy. "Have a seat. I'll see what I can do."

Mary Kate turned and walked to the chair she'd indicated, self-consciously straightening her suede jacket and contrasting scarf before she lowered herself onto the cushion. Glancing down at her straight wool skirt, she made sure her lacy slip wasn't peeking out the slit. She ran her fingers over her thick hair, trying to smooth it, and as usual, gave up with a sigh. Experience had shown her there was no use trying to wear her unruly locks any way but loose.

After a brief check for runs in her stockings, Mary Kate nodded her satisfaction. Without a doubt she looked the part of a mature, efficient, career-minded young woman. Now, all she needed was a little Irish luck.

"Damn." Flynn tossed his ink pen on the massive mahogany desk and his quarterly report into the metal wastebasket. He got to his feet and reached up, loosening his tie, slipping out of his jacket. He glanced at his watch, noting that it was only eleven o'clock. He had six hours to go until closing time—six long hours before he could get into his Jeep, drive the twenty-some-odd miles to Boulder and put to rest, once and for all, his irrational fears about love potions and red-haired fairies.

He would prove to himself that Friday night's fiasco was the result of Tex's idealistic theories about love at first sight by walking into O'Malley's Pub, finding Mary Kate, and... And what? he couldn't help but wonder. Attacking? Making a total jerk of himself again? Flynn stared out the window and shook his head, once again reliving that humiliating evening. Never in his life had he resorted to stealing kisses from unsuspecting females. It was mortifying. And he intended to apologize. Then he would get the hell back out of Mary Kate's life so she could get the hell out of his.

He would be back in control of the situation—able to get a good night's sleep again. He would vanquish to the far corners of his mind those ridiculous thoughts of marriage and babies that now haunted him—thanks, no doubt, to Tex. Such thoughts threatened his satisfaction with his single life-style. And he couldn't have that—not that he intended to be a bachelor forever; he really didn't. But he *did* plan on being much older before he finally settled down.

Flynn abruptly decided that what he actually needed to do that night was to get out his little black book, call up one of his standbys and glory in the advantages of being a bachelor.

"Mr. Rafferty?"

Flynn whirled at the sound of Carol Charleston's voice. She was Tex's younger sister and had the same blond hair and sunny disposition. Always under Tex's watchful eye since their parents were dead, she worked days at his office and attended business college at night. "Yes?"

"I have a loan applicant out front. Can you spare a few minutes?"

"Can't he come back Wednesday?" Flynn asked with a frown. The last thing he needed in his befuddled state was to have to deal with the technicalities of a loan application.

"*She* took off work to come in," the petite woman responded.

That figured. Flynn sighed in resignation and reached for his tailored jacket, slipping back into it before he readjusted his tie. Business was business, and though he didn't normally deal with clients anymore, he could, if necessary. Though well-off financially, thanks to his stepdad leaving everything in tip-top shape when he retired five years ago, Flynn was still in no position to turn away potential customers. "Send her in."

He took the application, never even looking down at it as he waited by the window, tapping an agitated thump on the plush carpet. He heard voices in the hallway outside and walked toward the door, stumbling over his own two feet when Mary Kate entered the room.

Flynn's stomach turned a backflip. He took a deep breath, closing his eyes for a moment in the hope Mary Kate O'Connor was a mirage that would disappear. But she was still standing in the doorway when he got up the nerve to look again—every bit as sexy, gorgeous and irresistible as he'd remembered. Flynn took a long, hard look and surrendered his bachelorhood to her. Then he got a grip on himself and snatched it back. Drawn like a magnet, he edged closer to Mary Kate, who gaped at him from the doorway.

Mary Kate's eyes locked with his. Suddenly she knew why she hadn't been able to get Flynn's kiss out of her head. He was utterly magnificent—a living, breathing temptation— the kind of man women gave up careers for. Mary Kate panicked. She grabbed the arm of the receptionist, who'd turned to leave. "Don't go."

Startled by the request, Carol froze, glancing from Mary Kate to Flynn, who now stood less than a yard away, sinfully handsome in his tailored suit.

"My phone's ringing," she said, stepping out into the hall. With that, she shut the door behind her, leaving Mary Kate and Flynn alone. Mary Kate swallowed hard. She threw out a hand to halt Flynn, who'd taken another ominous step toward her. "Stop where you are, buster."

He did, protesting, "I'm not going to touch you, I swear." As though to demonstrate his sincerity, Flynn put his hands behind him, adding, "I want to apologize for the way I acted Friday night and promise you it won't happen again."

"You're damned right it won't," she responded hotly, lashing out to hide her breathlessness. "You had no right to kiss me like that."

"I did catch you off guard, didn't I?" he admitted. "Next time *you* can do the honors."

The memory of that kiss sent Mary Kate's libido into hyperdrive. Her gaze dropped to his dark mustache and the full bottom lip peeking out from under it. The male smell of him tantalized her, lured her. She wondered fleetingly if he could possibly *know* how that brief caress haunted her nights—how much she *had* thought about kissing him again.

"There isn't going to be any next time," she found strength to reply. She whirled, managing two steps toward the door before he caught her arm in his hand.

"Where are you going?" he demanded, stepping in front of her, blocking her exit.

"Home."

"But Carol said you were applying for a loan."

"I've changed my mind," she snapped, embarrassingly breathless and scared to death he would realize it. She twisted free, adding, "You wouldn't give it to me anyway."

"How do you know?" he protested.

"Because every bank this side of the continental divide has already turned me down." She was two feet from escape now, poised for the dash to safety.

"They have?" Flynn glanced down at the application, frowning. "Surely things can't be that bad. I'm sure *we* can work something out."

Mary Kate gasped. "You go to hell," she exploded, dead certain she knew just what kind of "something" he had in mind.

She ducked past him, charging the short distance to the door and flinging it open, even as he called, "I just meant we could bend the rules a little. I own—" the door slammed, shaking the pictures on the walls ''—the company.'' He winced. ''Well, damn.''

Flynn, still stunned by his prediction that there would be a ''next time'' for them, didn't try to follow her. He walked back to his desk and sank into the chair, staring at the application without seeing it, as baffled by his own behavior over the last few minutes as he was by hers.

Why had she overreacted like that? Did she think he was some kind of lech who routinely seduced female clients? It looked like it, and all he really was trying to do was to explain that he often took gambles, loaning money to people no bank would seriously consider. And he'd been burned few times in his career—a fact he attributed to his innate ability to judge character.

Flynn sighed and turned his attention to the form in his hand, skipping right down to the reason why she needed a loan: to open a flower shop in Longmont. He scanned the figures she'd set down, noting that her estimates for starting up such a business seemed low to his expert eye—an indication she might be just a little naive regarding such matters.

Flynn's gaze returned to the top of the application and he began to read it more carefully. He saw Mary Kate's age and frowned. He'd assumed she was older than that. He read further, noting with interest that she held down two jobs—one as manager of a flower shop in Boulder and the second as a waitress at O'Malley's. She'd written that she intended to quit the day job and stay with the other one, no doubt to keep up payments on her credit card, which appeared to be charged to the limit.

He shook his head. No wonder the larger financial institutions had turned her down. Besides a two-year business degree, she had little to offer an investor. So why did he have this irrepressible urge to lend her the money? And what had happened to his big plans to say goodbye?

Flynn leaned back in his leather chair, whistling softly through his teeth when he suddenly remembered Tex's words: *She came, she saw, she conquered.* Was that what had happened to Flynn, too? Was there something to this love-at-first-sight stuff? Panic welled inside him.

A frown knit his dark brows. He needed some advice, and he needed it quickly. Unfortunately, the someone with whom he usually shared his problems was now on a honeymoon, of all things, and not due back in town until Wednesday.

That was the day after tomorrow, and in the interim, Flynn decided, it might be prudent to stay well clear of the red-haired, spell-weaving beauty who'd just stormed out of his office.

Outside, Mary Kate finally reached her car. She jumped into it, locking the door behind her. Her gloved fingers fumbled with the keys before she managed to insert the right one in the ignition and start the motor, causing a blast of frigid Colorado air to bathe her sheer-stockinged legs. Shivering, Mary Kate reached out, quickly shutting off the heater that would be nonfunctional until she was halfway home. How she longed for some warm Arizona sunshine to soothe the chill bumps that were now a permanent part of her anatomy.

She glanced nervously in the rearview mirror, half expecting Flynn to materialize behind her. Their latest encounter had unnerved her more than she'd ever believed possible, and it wasn't mere anger that made her heart flutter, her hands shake. Not that she didn't have every right to be angry. She did.... Or did she? Mary Kate ruthlessly suppressed a niggling doubt that she might have overreacted just a little. Clearly he thought her naive enough to believe he would give her the loan, no strings attached. Well, she wasn't *that* dumb. Every bank in the area had already turned her down. She knew he would have to do some fast talking to get any board of directors to agree to lend her money, and no doubt he would expect a few favors in return for his efforts.

What a jerk. And yet she'd never been so attracted to a male. Her irrational, totally feminine response to Flynn distressed her beyond belief, threatened her self-esteem. She'd always considered herself a sensible, career-oriented woman—had taken pride in the fact that she had her life so neatly mapped out. She'd believed no man could tempt her, confuse her. Obviously she'd been wrong. Obviously she'd inherited a weak gene from her mother—a gene that made her especially susceptible to sexy Irishmen.

Mary Kate shook her head and reached down to put the car in reverse. She eased the vehicle out of the parking space and then forward to the edge of the lot. After checking for oncoming traffic, she pulled out onto the boulevard, intent on getting as far away from Flynn as possible.

I can handle this, she assured herself. *I'm in control of my destiny.* Then she sent heavenward a heartfelt prayer that she would never, ever see him again.

Flynn was waiting for Tex the minute he strolled through the office door Friday morning, twenty minutes late.

"It's about time you got back," he grumbled.

As usual, Tex ignored the sarcasm, flashing him a lazy grin. "Well, good morning to you, too," he responded. He then turned to his sister, who was sitting at her desk. "Morning, kiddo. Have you made the coffee yet?"

"The coffee's been ready since nine, *when the office opened,*" Flynn snapped. When Tex raised an eyebrow in surprise, Flynn flushed. "I'm sorry. I've got a problem—need your help. Grab yourself a cup of coffee and come in my office."

"I'll be right there," Tex assured him, adding, "And I was late because I had to drop Jessie by the university. I underestimated the traffic."

"Forget it," Flynn replied. He stuck out his hand in apology, grinning sheepishly. "I'm glad you're finally back."

Tex shook the proffered hand. "So am I. And thanks for giving me that extra two days when I called." He grinned. "Aspen was great." Tex headed toward the coffeepot, sitting on a credenza in the corner. A second later he turned back, raising his mug to take a drink, but then halted abruptly, his eyes wide. "Would you look at that!"

Flynn followed the direction of his gaze, blinking in surprise when he spied the plant on Carol's desk. He walked over and picked up the pot, turning it this way and that to peruse the tiny, half-opened leaves that now adorned the unusually short stems. "My God, Carol, how'd you manage this?"

Blushing, Carol leaped to her feet. "It was that redhead who was in here Monday. She did it."

"Mary Kate did this?" Flynn demanded in disbelief.

"Mary Kate?" Tex echoed in surprise. "O'Connor?"

Flynn nodded mutely, staring at the healthy green plant, not quite believing the miracle.

"She cut off the old leaves," Carol told him, adding, "Then she talked to it."

"She did what?" Flynn asked, bobbling the pot in his agitation.

Carol reached across the desk, taking the plant from him and setting it carefully back down. "Talked to it—in a foreign language. It sounded singsongy, like a poem or a—"

"Spell?" Flynn asked, a little shiver of alarm traveling up his spine in spite of himself. Had Mary Kate bewitched his shamrock? Of course not. The Gaelic folktales he'd heard all his life—the ones involving curses, spells and love po-

tions—were just that: tales. There were no wee folk or lep-
rechauns in Colorado. Contrary to everything his
superstitious grandparents had ever told him, redheaded
colleens did not possess magical powers.

Or did they?

"My office," he told Tex, brushing past the grinning
blonde to lead the way down the hall. "Now."

The phone was ringing when Mary Kate entered her
apartment Friday afternoon after work. She tossed down
her purse, lunging for the jangling instrument in the half
hope it was O'Malley, her boss, telling her not to come in
tonight. She needed the money, but she needed a break just
as badly. Beginning with that disaster on Monday, the week
had been stressful. She'd been counting on getting that loan
from Tex. Now it looked like she was back to square one and
with nowhere to turn. Worse, Flynn had been on her mind
every waking minute, not to mention a few sleeping ones.
She was exhausted.

"Hello?"

"Flynn here. We need to talk." That familiar voice sent
shivers skittering down Mary Kate's spine. She closed her
eyes, a gesture that did little to erase the vivid mental image
of how good he'd looked the last time they were face-to-
face. Face-to-face? Trust her to think of *that* tempting scenario.

"You've said more than enough," she told him, quickly
moving to replace the receiver in its cradle.

"Don't hang up!"

Mary Kate heard the plea and hesitated fatally, slowly
raising the phone back up to her ear. "There's nothing you
could possibly say to make me change my mind about you,"
she warned.

"Not even 'I'm holding a check and it has your name on
it'?" Mary Kate's knees turned to putty. Dumbstruck, she

sank down on the couch. How on earth had he convinced his directors to give her the loan? And just what did he want in return? "Mary Kate?"

"I don't need your money," she informed him with difficulty, nearly choking on the lie. She did need it—badly—and no one else was going to lend it to her except maybe her very bossy dad—humiliation an independent young woman like Mary Kate couldn't tolerate. It took every ounce of strength she had to add, "The interest payments are too high."

"How do you know that?" Flynn countered softly. "You haven't even heard the terms."

Mary Kate's face flamed as did her temper when she thought of what those terms probably encompassed. "Like I told you Monday, you can go to—"

"This isn't a proposition," he interrupted. "At least not the kind you think. Why don't I come to the pub tonight? We'll talk."

She paled at the thought. "No, no, and another no. I don't want your money and I don't want to see you ever again. Is that understood?"

All she heard was the steady hum of a dial tone.

It was lucky for Mary Kate that O'Malley's Pub had attracted less than the usual Friday-night crowd that evening. She was a nervous wreck, having spilled a whole mug of beer, dropped a box of straws, and waited on someone else's table. One eye was always on the door, and the sight of Flynn walking through it at ten minutes to midnight, dissolved what remained of her composure. He was awesome in his form-hugging jeans, maroon sweater and leather aviator jacket. How could any female resist such a hunk?

Flynn nodded to O'Malley, who was standing in his usual spot at the cash register, and then headed across the bar, seating himself unerringly at one of Mary Kate's tables. She drew a shaky breath, grabbed a menu and a glass of water and walked to the table.

He watched her approach, his eyes sweeping her from curls to pumps in an appreciative appraisal that did amazing things to her heart rate. "Evening," he said when she reached him.

"I told you not to come here," she whispered, ever mindful of her employer, who watched with uncharacteristic interest. Her shaking fingers barely managed to set the goblet on the table. Then she handed him the menu.

He pushed it aside. "Have you eaten dinner?" he asked her.

"I want you to leave," she responded through gritted teeth. "Now."

"I haven't yet, and I'm starved," he told her, ignoring her request. He glanced at his watch. "You should be getting off in another ten minutes or so. Why don't we order a pizza to go, and eat it at your place?"

"Dammit, Flynn—" she exploded.

"Is something wrong?" O'Malley's question startled Mary Kate, who hadn't heard him approach.

"Nothing's wrong," she assured her employer hastily. "Mr. Rafferty is just leaving."

"Not before we talk," Flynn interjected. He turned to O'Malley, sticking out his hand. "Flynn Rafferty, Advantage Finance Company of Denver. I need to speak with Ms. O'Connor about a money matter. Do you have someplace we could talk for a moment—someplace private?"

"Use my office," O'Malley replied, much to Mary Kate's surprise. He glared at her, successfully silencing the refusal hovering on her lips with his gruff "We don't want any trouble here, O'Connor."

''But there's no troub—'' Flynn had risen to his feet and grasped her arm, leading her firmly in the direction O'Malley had indicated. When they reached the office, he pushed her inside and followed, shutting the door behind him.

Chapter Three

Mary Kate heard that ominous click and whirled, fists clenched, the fighting Irish in her riled. *"How could you?"* she demanded. And then she lunged for him, ready to do battle. Strong arms immediately engulfed her. Maroon knit smothered the rest of her opinion of him.

"Temper, temper," he cautioned. "I'm bigger than you are." Mary Kate heard something suspiciously like mirth in his voice and bristled. How dare he come to the pub when she'd told him not to! How dare he cast aspersions on her character and then *laugh* when she got angry!

Belatedly remembering a self-defense tactic one of her older brothers had taught her, Mary Kate tried to twist free. He didn't respond as anticipated, however, merely tightening his embrace, a move that flattened Mary Kate's full breasts against the unyielding wall of his chest. His body heat permeated the thin fabric of her costume. His jeans felt rough against her legs.

She closed her eyes and gulped, desperately clinging to her temper, which was fading fast in the wake of another, more powerful emotion. Acutely aware of Flynn's lips, mere millimeters away, it was all she could do not to raise her face and take back the kiss he'd stolen from her several nights ago. Clearly that traitorous gene of her mother's was at work again, boggling her mind, stealing her ire, making her want this man she loathed.

Loathed? Not *that*, exactly; in fact, not that at all. If they had met five years from now, he would be the one struggling to escape. But it wasn't five years from now, and dedicated career woman that she was, Mary Kate didn't want or need these distracting feelings of desire.

"Let me go," she demanded.

"Only if you promise to hear me out. I have a plan, and it's a good one."

I'm in control, she told herself sternly, taking several deep breaths. She ignored the sweaty palms and rapid pulse that defied her claim. Clearly, if she wanted to put some distance between the two of them, she would have to agree to listen to whatever Flynn had to say. He showed no inclination to let her go, and many more minutes in this precarious position just might prove to be her demise, not to mention his. "I promise."

He leaned back slightly so he could get a better look at her face. His dark eyes studied her, reading her motives. Gradually he loosened his hold and stepped away from her.

Mary Kate sagged with relief and tried to salvage what remained of her temper. Easing around Flynn until she was near the door, she then leaned on it, feeling a little more secure. "You've got a lot of nerve, coming in and giving O'Malley the impression I've got money problems. I could lose my job, for heaven's sake. Now I want you to go out there and tell him this whole thing was a stupid joke."

"Don't be mad, Mary Kate. I admit that was a lousy thing to do, but I couldn't think of another way to get your undivided attention. Besides, what does the half owner of a flower shop need with a job as a barmaid, anyway?"

"What do you mean 'half owner of a flower shop'?" Mary Kate snapped, fast losing patience.

Flynn glanced at his watch. "I'll explain everything, but not here. It's midnight and the pub is closing down. Why don't we drive to that pizza parlor up the street, order a large one to go, and head for your apartment? We'll have our little talk there."

"We talk here or not at all," Mary Kate countered, dead certain her apartment was the last place she needed to be with the irresistible likes of Flynn Rafferty.

He sighed in exasperation. "Oh, all right, but you're going to have to learn to trust me. I won't attack again; I told you the next kiss was yours."

"Well, don't hold your breath waiting for it. I found the last one insulting."

"'Insulting'?" Flynn exclaimed, taking a step toward her.

"Damned insulting," Mary Kate qualified, bracing herself against his charm. "How would you like to be grabbed by a total stranger on your own front porch?"

Flynn grinned, leaning forward to cup her chin in his hand. "Why don't we go to my place and find out?"

"See?" Mary Kate exploded, slapping his hand away. "You're doing it again. Coming on to me like I was—"

"The most intriguing young woman I've ever encountered?" he interjected, his voice husky. "A fiery-haired enchantress who stole my heart the moment I first laid eyes on her?" He stepped even closer, his eyes narrowed in suspicion. "Did you put something in my drink last Friday night? A love potion, perhaps?"

She gasped. "Of course, I didn't."

Flynn winced, abruptly whirling and putting some distance between them as he walked across the office and perched on the edge of O'Malley's cluttered desk. He sighed heavily. "Well, something's wrong with me." He shook his head. "Every time you come near, I..." His eyes narrowed, "You aren't by any chance picking up on these vibes between us, are you?" She shook her head emphatically—*too* emphatically. He sighed again. "I thought not. If I promise to behave, can we get out of here and get on with this? I believe you're going to like what I have to say."

Curious in spite of herself, Mary Kate hesitated. She wanted to know what he'd meant by that "half owner" comment a second ago. Surely she would be safe enough in the pizza parlor up the street. They could order dinner and eat it there. "If you'll agree to eat at the restaurant and talk to me there, I'll go with you."

He leaped to his feet, grinning. "Get your coat."

Ten minutes later found them entering Luigi's, an all-night restaurant that was one of Mary Kate's favorite haunts. Many times since her arrival in Boulder, she and Jessica had grabbed a pizza after work and stayed up until all hours, talking and dreaming. It looked as though Jessica's dreams had come true. It looked as though Mary Kate's might not.

A waitress greeted them and led the way to a table in a shadowy corner of the room. Mary Kate noted with some surprise that the red-checkered tablecloth and the flaming taper, which flickered in the breeze of their arrival, were really quite romantic. This restaurant was perfect for a rendezvous, she realized, glancing uneasily at Flynn. She certainly hoped he didn't think she'd brought *him* here for that reason.

Flynn glanced around the room, liking what he saw. The table was cozy—perfect for two people who cared for one another. Too bad he and Mary Kate didn't qualify. Too bad? He actually thought it was too bad? Damn. He was in worse shape than he'd realized.

Not for the first time in the past few minutes, Flynn wondered just what he was doing here with Mary Kate, and why this crazy idea of his had seemed so reasonable this afternoon when he and Tex hashed it out. Shaking his head at the mysteries of life, Flynn assisted Mary Kate out of her coat. He smiled to himself when she shivered.

"Cold?" he asked when they were both seated.

She rubbed her bare arms briskly and shrugged. "Always."

"Since I'm hot-blooded, this area is perfect for me. I'd sure like to hear why you chose to live in a place with winters that rival the North Pole."

Mary Kate smiled at his exaggeration. "I needed a job, and fast. My cousin Shannon offered me one as manager of her flower shop. Since that fit in beautifully with my plans to own my own business, I jumped at the chance."

"Why the rush—to find a job, I mean?" Flynn couldn't help but ask, intrigued by her reply.

She hesitated and then said, "I knew if I didn't leave Phoenix, I'd murder one of my big brothers, or maybe even all of them."

"How many is 'all of them'?" Flynn asked, leaning back slightly so the waitress could hand him a menu and ice water.

Mary Kate took a sip of her own water and grinned. "Four."

Flynn whistled. "And why were you going to murder one or all of them?"

"It's a long, sad story," she warned him, all traces of amusement gone. She reached for her menu, raising it up in a move that hid all of her face except her emerald eyes, now glowing in the candlelight. Not for the first time since he'd met Mary Kate, Flynn's body responded to her delicate femininity. It was going to be a long night, he decided. He could only hope he would be able to keep his promise to keep his hands to himself.

"I'm in no hurry," he prompted gently.

"But I am."

"Then talk fast," he advised.

The waitress appeared at that moment to take their order. They agreed on a large pizza with everything on it, and after pouring Mary Kate a cup of steaming coffee, the waitress left them alone again. Mary Kate sipped the dark brew, sighed her pleasure and explained: "There's quite an age gap between me and my brothers. Mom was twenty-eight years old when she had her fourth son, thirty-five when I was born. I guess my brothers didn't quite know what to make of me. They've always been extremely over-protective, which was all right when I was little. But now that I'm all grown-up and fully capable of handling my own life—in particular my love life—it's a darned nuisance."

Flynn laughed heartily, thinking of his own little sister, who probably had the same complaint. Although pretty, Peg didn't have Mary Kate's striking good looks or shapely figure. Flynn could well imagine that Mary Kate's big brothers might look with suspicion on any man who came around. Thank goodness they were safe in Arizona. Or were they?

"Your brothers live in Phoenix?" he asked.

"Yes."

"Good." He grinned at the censure in her eyes and asked, "So what happened to make you move north?"

She shrugged, not speaking until the waitress, who'd just appeared again, set salads in front of them. "My mother and dad are in Ireland visiting relatives and will be for several more months. They're helping my grandmother sort out my granddad's affairs. He died recently.'' Flynn noticed her misty eyes before she looked down at her plate.

He reached out, taking her hand in his and squeezing it gently. "I'm sorry."

Mary Kate shrugged self-consciously, easing her fingers free of his. "He was a dear old man, and though I never got to see him much, I'll still miss him." She sighed and dipped her fork into her salad. "Anyway, my brothers began to haunt me the minute my mother left the States. They're all spoiled rotten, even the married ones, expecting free laundry service, free meals, free baby-sitting. Not that I don't love every one of my seven nieces and nephews—I really do. And I don't mind helping my brothers out every now and then, but there are limits.

"Then Shawn—he's the brother closest in age to me—dropped by my apartment one night when I had a guest over for dinner. Not only did he invite himself to eat, he was unspeakably rude to Joe, my date, hinting that he had no business being in my apartment. I'm twenty-one years old for God's sake! I was so embarrassed. I could have killed him—I almost did after Joe got fed up and left."

Flynn bit his lip to keep from laughing at her outrage. "So you called your cousin, packed your bags and flew the coop?"

"Something like that."

"And your brothers haven't come after you yet?"

"Alan—he's the oldest—drove up to check things out. I sent him packing, and quick."

Flynn *did* laugh then, his sympathies with Alan. "Do you like Boulder?"

"It's all right." Their waitress approached, this time bearing a pizza, steamy hot and savory. Mary Kate's face lit up. She reached for a piece, licking a smear of sauce off her fingers with a flick of her tongue. Flynn had to look away, swallowing convulsively. "I believe you said you were from

Paducah. Was it really the winters that enticed you to Colorado?"

"I moved here because I was too young to have a say when my father decided to leave Kentucky. I stay here because my stepdad sold me his finance company when he retired."

"Are you saying that you *own* Advantage Finance Company?" Mary Kate gasped.

"That's right."

"So you can pretty much set your own guidelines—for loans, I mean?"

He nodded again, smiling at her growing excitement. "I can."

Mary Kate lay down her pizza, wiped her hands on a napkin and leaned forward, propping her chin in her palm as she assimilated this revelation. Flynn owned the company. He made his own rules—didn't have to answer to anyone. That meant he could give her a loan if he wanted, and that there really might not be any strings attached. "Why on earth didn't you tell me?"

"I tried, honey. You were so sure I was out to get you, I couldn't finish a sentence."

"Don't call me—"

"'Honey'? Then how about 'partner' instead?" He leaned across the table, planting his elbows on either side of his plate. "I have a proposition for you—one that I believe will benefit both of us. Want to hear it?"

"Start talking," she replied.

Flynn drew a deep breath and plunged ahead. "I looked at your application and at the figures you provided. I think they're too low."

"But they're not," she hastily assured him. "I've done a lot of research. I'm sure I've thought of everything."

He shook his head slowly, hating to disillusion her. "I foresee problems. What if you don't find a building with rent as cheap as you've counted on?"

"I have the building all picked out," she countered. "I've even talked with the owner. It'll need a few modifications, but I thought I could do most of them myself...." Her voice trailed off into silence. She could tell by Flynn's dubious expression that he thought her naive; and that rankled. "What else was wrong?"

He hesitated fractionally and then replied, "You'll need twice the amount of liability insurance you've quoted."

"Twice?" she echoed in disbelief.

"At least that. And what about a delivery van? You'll have to buy one, you know."

"What's wrong with my car?" she asked, frowning. "It's practically new, and I've replaced the dead battery. Besides, it's a station wagon and should do fine for a while."

"You'll put needless miles on it. And besides, how will your automobile-insurance carrier feel about your letting a total stranger drive it?"

"But *I'm* going to make the deliveries," she exclaimed.

"How are you going to manage that?" he countered. "Some flowers will have to be delivered during working hours. Are you going to close down the shop while you go hopping all over town?"

"Just for a while. I won't be able to afford any paid help the first few months." Mary Kate's eyes brimmed with tears of frustration, which she blinked away. She'd had just about enough of Flynn's condescending attitude. "Give me some credit. I majored in business administration—graduated with honors. I'm no fool."

Flynn sighed and reached out, capturing her hand in his. "I never said you were. What I am saying is that we have a little problem here. But don't worry. I have a solution, too." He released her and began to search his pockets for the piece of paper he'd labored over Wednesday afternoon and most of Thursday. "I've worked up some new totals." He pointed to some numbers at the bottom of the paper. "That's the new loan figure I've come up with."

Mary Kate glanced at it, gasping when she read the amount—nearly three times what she'd thought she could manage on. "Mother McCrea!" she stormed. "I'll never be able to borrow that much money—much less pay it back."

"Now, don't get excited," he soothed, taking the offending piece of paper away and tucking it back into his shirt pocket.

"'Don't get excited'?" she exclaimed, biting her now trembling lip. Suddenly not hungry anymore, she scooted her chair back and leaped to her feet. "Unless you've got a miracle up your sleeve, there's no point in even continuing this conversation," she retorted, self-consciously swiping away a tear that had brimmed over to snake its way down her cheek.

"Hear me out. It'll just take a minute," he urged, adding softly, "Your pizza's getting cold."

Dutifully she sat back down and picked up the pizza.

"Now," Flynn then continued, "it's my business to make investments—usually in the form of simple loans, much like the one you wanted. But that's not the only way I work."

Mary Kate sighed in exasperation. "I'm not a simpleton, Flynn. I know how investors make money."

"Of course, you do," he hastily agreed. "So I'll get right to the point. Currently I'm part owner of a doughnut shop, a laundromat and a Chinese restaurant. Since the first of the year, I've been on the lookout for another good investment, and I'd be more than willing to sink some capital into a flower shop—for a percentage of the profits, of course."

"What are you saying to me?" Mary Kate asked, not quite believing her ears.

"I want to be your partner. I'll provide the cash and the brains; you can provide the—"

"Green thumb?" Mary Kate interjected wryly, somehow managing to hold her ever-faithful temper in check. Obviously, Flynn thought she was a total fluff-head with nothing to offer a viable business, and even less brains. Well, her estimates might have been a little low, but his were ridiculously high. No doubt he'd inflated the figures, thinking she would be so overwhelmed by his generosity that she would fall right into his arms.

Oblivious to her rising indignation, Flynn grinned. "You have one of those, for a fact. You worked a miracle on that shamrock of mine. It's come back to life. I think that's what really made me decide to give you your shop."

"There's not going to be any shop."

Flynn stiffened in disbelief, his jaw dropping. "Why not?"

"Because I don't take charity," she snapped.

"What charity?"

"Your offer to subsidize an airhead like me."

"I never said you were an airhead," he protested, clearly startled. "And I'm not offering to 'subsidize' you, either. Believe me, you'll earn every cent you get from me."

"I can imagine," she retorted coldly. "Well, for your information, I am not in the market for a partner—business or otherwise." Mary Kate got to her feet again, standing tall, shoulders squared, chin high. "I may have had a little trouble getting a loan so far, but I am by no means desperate enough to hook up with the likes of you. I *will* get the money I need, even if I have to resort to borrowing it from my dad. And there *won't* be any strings attached when I do." With that, she snatched her coat and strode to the front door. Flynn caught her before she could step through it.

He grabbed her arm and turned her to face him. "Dammit, Mary Kate, you're the most infuriating—" He took a deep breath and started over. "You're jumping to conclusions. Have I said one thing—one *single* thing—to make you think this will be more than a business arrangement? Now, have I?"

Mary Kate pulled on her jacket and glared at him. "Monday you said we could 'work something out.'"

"And that's what I'm trying to do," he replied. "I think a partnership will benefit both of us."

Undaunted, Mary Kate tried again. "On the phone you talked about 'terms.'"

"Any business arrangement has 'terms.' That's a legal phrase. Surely you've heard it before." He cocked his head, eyes narrowed. "You know what your problem is?"

"No, and I don't want you to tell me," she retorted, pivoting to walk toward the exit.

Flynn rolled his eyes in exasperation, almost ready to give up and let her go. The sight of her long legs and gently swaying hips immediately banished that idea to regions unknown, however.

"You've inherited a double dose of Irish stubborn, that's what," he called after her, his words echoing in the empty foyer. "And it won't let you admit you just might be wrong about me." Mary Kate gasped, whirling to stalk back to him.

"If you hadn't jumped me Friday night, I might find it a little easier to believe you," she snapped.

"So *that's* it," Flynn said. He shook his head with impatience. "I promised the next move would be yours, didn't I? What more do you want?" His eyes narrowed.

"What do you mean?"

"I think maybe I'm not the only one having problems when we two get together. I think maybe you *do* feel something between us and you're afraid of what will happen if we join forces—spend a lot of time together."

Mary Kate blanched at the accuracy of his guess. "There's nothing between us," she lied. "And even if there were, I wouldn't let a little thing like that stand in the way of a sound business venture."

"So that's settled," Flynn said. "Now are you going to forgive me for that one little slipup last Friday or not? I sure hate to see you lose the chance of a lifetime—and all over some stupid misunderstanding."

Mary Kate chewed her bottom lip, trying to decide what to do. He was right about losing the chance of a lifetime. In spite of her brave words to the contrary, she doubted that she would ever get another opportunity like this one. A partnership was better than nothing, and if she played her cards right, might even be exactly what she needed at this point in her career. "Just how much control would you expect to maintain over the flower shop—*if* we were partners, I mean? I want to be more than a manager, you know."

"Hey, it would be your baby," he assured her airily. "I might offer a *little* advice every now and then, but that's all."

Mary Kate sighed her indecision. "I'm tired and hungry and I can't decide without more information."

"I understand," he said. "Why don't I have the waitress pack the pizza to go so you can take it home?"

"I'm going alone," she warned.

"Of course," Flynn replied. "You get some rest and tomorrow I'll come by your place so we can work out the details."

"Let's meet someplace instead," she countered smoothly.

Flynn shook his head at her stubbornness, but gave in. "All right. Nine o'clock?"

"Make that ten—at the waffle house on Roosevelt Road," she told him, rewarded for her obstinacy by his grimace.

But all he said was "I'll be there."

He arrived minutes after she did the next morning, dressed in cords and a light ski jacket that hugged his broad chest. Mary Kate, already seated at a booth in the restaurant, watched him get out of the Jeep and shivered for him, wondering how he kept from freezing in the icy wind. Then she remembered his observation that he was hot-blooded. Was that the same thing as hot-natured? she wondered, losing that thought when he approached her table, smiling that smile of his.

His eyes swept her and began to twinkle as he noted her thick woolen sweater, jeans and knee-high boots. "This is the first time I've seen you dressed for the weather," he commented, slipping into the bench seat across the table from her.

She laughed, knowing that was true. "This is how I look most of the time. You should see what I sleep in."

"I'm game."

The reply was silky soft, tantalizing. Mary Kate's eyes locked with his. "You're doing it again," she warned.

"That just slipped out," he protested earnestly. He snatched up the grease-stained menu tucked between the saltshaker and the napkin holder at one end of the table. "Have you eaten?"

"Leftover pizza," she replied.

Flynn grinned and ordered a cup of coffee and a stack of pancakes from the waitress who'd approached. When they were alone again, he asked, "Did you think about my proposition?"

"Yes, I did," Mary Kate replied, silently adding *all night long*. "And I've decided it might not be such a bad idea."

"Hot dog!" His flattened palm came down on the wooden table, jarring it.

"I want to hear all the terms, and as soon as you finish your breakfast, I'm going to take you to the building I've selected and see what you think."

"All right," he agreed, smiling at her.

Flynn had slept little the night before, his body tensed, his mind reliving his latest volatile encounter with Mary Kate. He'd experienced serious second thoughts about the wisdom of this partnership, but reassured himself that it was gut instinct and Mary Kate's amazing green thumb that had made him want to give her a chance to make a go of her shop, and not at all any kind of spell. It wasn't as if he wanted to get involved with her; he really didn't. He was happy playing the field, and he intended to cling to his bachelor ways for many years to come.

Things are going well, Mary Kate decided, smiling back at him. If the terms of this partnership were halfway reasonable, she would accept Flynn's offer and open her shop in Longmont, over thirty-five miles from Denver. She would make all the decisions, be in control, succeed. She wouldn't lose her heart, and therefore her identity, to some man before she wanted to, and her life would continue along its carefully-thought-out, neatly planned course.

Chapter Four

In forty-five minutes, the two of them were in Mary Kate's car, maneuvering the snow-patched streets of Longmont. Though not really that familiar with the city, Flynn could nonetheless tell when they left the main business district and entered a semiresidential section. His trained eye noted that the real estate here was not nearly as valuable as in other areas or as well kept. He frowned thoughtfully, wondering just where Mary Kate was headed. As far as he was concerned, they were already on the wrong side of the tracks and still rolling.

When she finally pulled into the minuscule, snow-crusted drive of a tiny brick building, Flynn cringed, holding back his groan of dismay with difficulty. This utterly plain structure, in the middle of a less-than-satisfactory neighborhood, would never do. Why, he would lose sleep worrying that she might be working late in this part of town.

"Well, what do you think?" Mary Kate turned to him to ask.

"This place is a dump," Flynn replied, practicing his usual tact.

"It is not!" she immediately retorted, glaring at him. Then she glanced back toward the building. "Well, maybe it is . . . now. But it has definite possibilities."

"You can't be serious," Flynn moaned. "Not only is the building too small, so is the drive. Your customers will have to park at that grocery store across the street and walk over."

Mary Kate looked out the window, pursing her lips thoughtfully, "Couldn't we enlarge the drive?"

"Only if you can talk your neighbors into donating part of their backyard. *Really*, Mary Kate, you can't . . ."

She tuned out the rest of his holier-than-thou lecture, opening the car door and getting out to ventilate some of her irritation by slamming it behind her. Trust him to see the *im*possibilities instead of the possibilities, she fumed, remembering the weekends she'd spent combing the city looking for an affordable location for her business. This former shoe-repair shop was the pick of the lot, if a little dowdy, and would be adequate for her needs with only minor modifications. That was a big plus and far outweighed the disadvantages of location and size.

Mary Kate stomped through the snow to the front door, quickly inserting into the lock a key she'd obtained earlier that morning from the owner. She heard the slam of Flynn's door, but never looked back as she entered the deserted building, which reeked of some kind of chemical.

Since all the windows inside were sealed, she left the door open to let in some air and sunlight while she made her way across the debris-littered floor to open the drapes. She closed her eyes against the cloud of dust that sifted downward, opening them again when Flynn's choking cough came from directly behind her. Mary Kate turned to face him.

"There are two rooms, not counting the bath," she explained, as though he were as enthused about this project as she. "This one is the biggest, just right for displays, a refrigerated showcase and—"

"Just right?" Flynn echoed in disbelief, cutting off the rest of her sentence. "*Just right?* Open your eyes, honey. You'd be lucky to get a cash register and a table in this room, much less a cooler of any size. Surely you can see this will never work."

Mary Kate threw up her arms in exasperation. "Don't call me 'honey.' And if you're talking about our partnership, I can only agree—it *will* never work."

"I'm talking about this building," Flynn said. "The success of our partnership isn't even in question, and neither is the success of your flower shop—once we find the proper location for it, that is." He glanced around the room, shaking his head. "Even if we could get this place set up to suit us, you'd outgrow it in six months. Come on. Think big."

"Just how big are we talking?" Mary Kate asked, tilting her head slightly and frowning at him.

He shrugged. "Certainly bigger than this."

Mary Kate sighed, seeing the wisdom of his expectations in spite of herself. "And just where am I supposed to find this bigger building? There's not that much commercial property available around here, you know."

"Then let's go somewhere else," Flynn suggested. "What about Denver, my stomping grounds? I have some friends in real estate and some rental property of my o—" He broke off, his eyes widening with inspiration. "I've got it! The perfect solution."

"Call the whole thing off?" Mary Kate interjected wryly.

"Not that," Flynn responded. "I own a house that's sitting smack dab in the middle of an oversized lot that would be perfect for the shop. It's close to both business and residential areas and in a good part of town. Why don't we go take a look at it?''

''You mean set up my shop in a house?''

''No. I mean tear down the house and build exactly what you want. I was going to raze it eventually, anyway, to put up office buildings or maybe a laundromat. Why not build our shop instead?''

''That'll cost too much . . .'' Mary Kate objected, though her head had begun to spin at the very idea of opening a brand-new shop she had designed.

''But we'll *own* it,'' Flynn rightly argued.

Mary Kate stood in silence, thinking big in spite of herself. ''Denver, huh?'' she finally murmured.

''Denver,'' he said with a brisk nod. ''Just twenty-six miles away—not so very far for you to drive every day.''

''I guess it wouldn't hurt to take a look at it,'' she said, turning to head back out the door, Flynn one step behind. When they got into the car she glanced at the gas gauge, commenting, ''I'll have to get some gasoline before we go, but it'll just take a minute.''

''We'll take the Jeep instead,'' Flynn told her. ''I have a full tank, and besides, we have to go right by the restaurant where I left it parked.''

Mary Kate hesitated, hating to give up the independence of using her own car—even if she didn't enjoy driving on icy highways. ''We're going straight there and straight back, right?''

Flynn nodded and swore, ''Scout's honor,'' only later recalling he'd never been one of those.

They covered the miles to Denver at an easy pace. By the time they reached the outskirts of the metropolis, Mary Kate had asked just enough questions about the rental property to elicit from Flynn the details of how he got into the investment business in the first place. It seemed he was the older of two children and had taken over the duties of temporary provider for his mother and sister at age eighteen, when his father deserted them.

His mother, who had always led a sheltered life, suffered a breakdown that lasted for several months before Flynn took charge, bullying her into seeking help from a family counselor. While she got her life back together, Flynn graduated from high school and got a well-paying job as a "repo man" for the owner of the loan company that was trying to collect on his runaway father's bad debts. He acted as both a mom and dad to his little sister, Peg, during those troubled times—a habit Mary Kate believed still prevailed, judging from the sound of things.

A year and a half later, Flynn's mother married his boss, who then packed him off to a college with a promise that if he came back with a degree in accounting he could one day take over Advantage Finance Company. It didn't surprise Mary Kate to learn that Flynn had managed that in three years, returning to work for his stepdad until the older man retired, at which time he bought him out.

In awe of Flynn's drive and his enviable success at such an early age, Mary Kate considered herself fairly warned that she might have her hands full maintaining equality in their partnership. Flynn had been taking care of his business and that of a few others for years, and clearly loved to be in control as much as she did. That boded ill for harmony between them.

Mary Kate said little once they entered the business district, her eager eyes taking in every detail of the city she'd visited only a few times since her move to Colorado. As always, she relished the beauty of the area and the backdrop of the majestic Rocky Mountains, utterly breathtaking under a blanket of early January snow.

Denver, once a gold-mining town and now a leader in electronics and space-age industry, was a picturesque blend of old and new, which intrigued Mary Kate. Flynn pointed out the sights of the city as he drove, also sharing some of its colorful past and revealing his love of his adopted state. Finally he turned the Jeep off the main thoroughfare onto a side street called Pinkerton Lane, driving for two blocks before he turned again. They had driven only a few yards before Mary Kate spotted a huge Victorian house that dominated the other dwellings and businesses on the street and looked as if it might have been built sometime around the late 1800s. Although the structure was obviously in a sad state of disrepair, Mary Kate, who loved anything old, could imagine how stately it might have been at one time.

"Slow down," she urged Flynn. "I want to get a better look at that house there on the right—that gorgeous, three-story one."

He grinned at her. "I'll do better than that," he said, turning onto the icy, graveled drive that led to it and crunching to a halt. He opened the door and stepped out, peering back in at Mary Kate when she didn't immediately move to follow suit. "Aren't you coming?"

"Where?" she asked, frowning.

"Inside the house to get a better look."

She came to life, reaching to open the door and scramble out of the Jeep. "The owner won't mind?"

"I *am* the owner," he told her, cupping her elbow with his hand to help her navigate the treacherous drive. "This is the house I was telling you about—the one I'm going to raze so we can build your shop."

She nearly tripped Flynn when she whirled to face him, green eyes wide in disbelief. "Are you insane? You can't destroy a house like this."

Flynn shrugged, feigning an indifference he didn't really feel. More than once since they'd left Longmont less than an hour ago, he'd had second thoughts about his impulsive offer to destroy this old house he'd owned the better part of a year. Flynn had accepted it as payment of a debt and had lost cash on the deal, though he'd never regretted it. The classic beauty of the mansion haunted him—the reason he'd let it sit idle all these months. Could it be he wouldn't have to tear down the structure, after all? he wondered. Did Mary Kate possess the enthusiasm, energy and eagerness necessary to restore it? The seldom acknowledged, embarrassingly romantic side of him fervently hoped so, while the financier side couldn't help but think of the massive amounts of time and money such a project would entail. "It's just an old building."

"Flynn Rafferty, you should be ashamed of yourself," Mary Kate scolded, shaking off his hand to maneuver the rest of the distance to the house alone. "It's much more than that." She paused just before she stepped on the ornately trimmed porch that bordered two sides of the sprawling house, throwing her head back so she could see clear to the weather vane on the uppermost peak of the tallest gable. Then she turned back to him, dramatically proclaiming, "It's history."

Flynn waited until she'd climbed the steps and disappeared around the corner of the porch before he allowed himself a smile of pleasure at her excitement. His smile grew even wider when she reappeared, calling "Hurry up, slowpoke" while she rattled the front doorknob.

He took the stairs two at a time, joining her on the porch and then following her inside the house after he unlocked the door. He let her explore at will and alone, chuckling to himself at her muted exclamations of discovery and delight, drifting back from the second floor and then the third. When she finally finished her tour and descended the stairs nearly half an hour later, it was to find him sitting sprawled on the steps, his eyes closed and his back against the wall, waiting for her.

Mary Kate hesitated on the landing just above Flynn, trying to think of the magic words that might dissuade him from his dastardly deed. But what could she say to convince him that this marvelous mansion with its secret staircases and hidey-holes was perfect for her flower shop?

Wordlessly she joined him there, easing herself down on the next step up. He turned his head slightly to face her and opened one eye, obviously aware that she was bursting with excitement and had something to say.

"Nice house," she commented, her tongue uncharacteristically tied.

"I've always thought so," Flynn admitted, much to her surprise. He had opened both eyes now and watched her intently. "Spill it, Mary Kate."

"Spill what?" she hedged, wondering yet again if he could read her thoughts.

"Whatever's on your mind."

She cleared her throat—a nervous sound to her own ears—and did just that. "I have an idea."

Flynn lowered his foot from the banister on which he'd propped it, uncrossed his arms from over his chest and shifted position enough to ease his considerable length up onto her step—a move that disconcerted Mary Kate. Desperate to keep her wits about her, she slid over fractionally, so their bodies wouldn't accidentally touch and ignite. Unfortunately she had no control over the air she breathed, air now fragrant with his spicy after-shave, and dizzyingly potent.

"Let's hear it," he said, leaning slightly forward to prop his elbows on his knees.

She swallowed hard, struggling to get her suddenly scattered ideas back in order. "How would you feel about my moving into your house?"

"How fast can you pack?" Flynn responded smoothly, even as Mary Kate's thoughtless choice of question echoed in her muddled brain.

She snorted her disgust at herself, hastily blurting, "Let me rephrase that. How would you feel about my moving into *this* house . . . specifically on the third floor?"

"Third floor, huh? Does that mean you have plans for the first and second, as well?" Flynn questioned, his face now serious.

"Yes," she agreed with an eager nod. "I want to restore this place—put my shop on the first floor and save the second for expansion."

"Do you have any idea how *big* a project that would be?"

Mary Kate, unperturbed, shrugged. "You *did* tell me to think that way."

"So I did." Flynn got to his feet, reaching down to pull Mary Kate to hers. "I can't make a decision like this in a drafty old house. There's a waffle house a few blocks away. Let's go hash this out there."

He descended the stairs, walking across the foyer and out the door before she caught up. Just before he stepped off the porch, she grabbed his arm, halting him.

"Flynn?"

"Hmm?" he responded, glancing back over his shoulder at her.

"Is there any chance at all I can talk you into this? Or have you already got a big fat 'No' on your mind?" Mary Kate asked, unable to tolerate the suspense until they got to the restaurant.

His solemn brown eyes locked with her pleading ones for just a moment before he shook his head, murmuring, "Apparently, where you're concerned, there's not a 'no' bone in my body."

Slowly the meaning of his words sank in. *Yes,* her mind sang. He'd said "Yes." With a squeal of joy, Mary Kate threw herself at Flynn, wrapping her arms around his neck, tugging his face down so she could plant her kiss of thanks right on his lips, which were now parted in a wheeze of surprise.

He stiffened initially, probably to keep from toppling off the porch, and then rallied, swaying forward to mold his body to hers. He deepened the kiss, his tongue teasing the soft fullness of her lips and then exploring the recesses of her mouth in a tantalizing caress that set her heart to thumping. Shocked by this heated response to what had begun as a spontaneous expression of gratitude, Mary Kate tipped her head back, gasping for air.

She could see Flynn was in no better shape, his rasping breaths plainly audible, the pulse in his neck jumping wildly. They stepped apart by mutual consent, each eyeing the other warily. The silence between them grew ominous.

"You kissed me," Flynn finally accused, unconsciously echoing her response to *his* attack mere nights before.

"You kissed me back," she countered, to hide her mortification that she had just attacked this near stranger and on his own front porch *after* reading him the riot act for doing the same thing.

"Isn't that exactly what you wanted?"

Mary Kate gaped at him. "What are you talking about?"

"Wasn't that kiss a promise of things to come—the little bonus I can expect every time I do what you want me to?"

She gasped at the insult. "How dare you!"

Flynn took a step toward her, his eyes narrowed dangerously. "Come on, Mary Kate. Be honest. Didn't you spot me in that bar and think, 'There's a sap if I ever saw one. One little kiss, and *he'll* loan me the money I need'?"

"You're crazy! I didn't even know who you were that night. Besides, you kissed me first."

"After you seduced me."

"*Me* seduce *you*?" She whirled, charging down the steps, and then pivoted abruptly to charge back up them, halting bare inches from him, her finger poked into his chest. "Mother McCrea, Flynn. I have my career to think of. I don't have time for such nonsense."

"And neither do I," Flynn snapped.

Mary Kate stared at him for a long, silent moment and then shook her head. "Do you *really* think I'm the kind of woman who'd use you to get ahead?"

Flynn sighed. "Not really. I guess I'm just trying to rationalize this crazy attraction I have for you."

"You're attracted to me?" Mary Kate asked.

"Mildly. I think."

"Well, I'll be darned," she said. "It just so happens I think I'm *mildly* attracted to you, too." Flynn's eyes flew open wide at her words. They stood in silence for a moment, gazes locked, and then he laughed—a sound that brought a frown to Mary Kate's face.

"What's so funny?" she demanded.

"Us," he told her, leaning back against the thick wooden post that supported the porch roof. "From the moment we met, I thought you were out to get me. All the time you thought I was out to get you. In reality, however, nobody's out to get anyone, even though we actually *think* we might be mildly attracted to each other. . . ."

"Stop," Mary Kate moaned, pressing her fingers to her temples. "You're giving me a headache."

Flynn grinned. "Let's go get some coffee." He reached for Mary Kate's hand, lacing his fingers through hers and pulling her after him down the steps to the waiting Jeep. Once they were seated inside it again, he turned to her and said, "You know who's really to blame for this confusion, don't you?"

"Who?"

"Tex. That traitor had no business falling in love. It shook my faith in truth, justice and the American way. It also scared the life out of me."

"I take it Tex was a 'confirmed bachelor,' too," Mary Kate dryly noted.

"Damned right he was. And one of the most dedicated. To this day I can't figure out what happened to make him change his mind."

"And what's all that got to do with you and me?"

"Just this. Since I'd been worrying about him for weeks, I was in a highly susceptible state when I met you—*love on the brain*," Flynn explained.

"That accounts for your reaction to me. What about my reaction to you?"

"Simple. You'd been worrying about Jessie, hadn't you?"

"Of course. She's only known Tex a very short time. How can she be so sure he's the one?"

"See there. You have love on the brain, too."

Mary Kate, lost in thought, chewed on her fingernail. "Oddly enough, that makes sense."

"Of course, it does. And if the truth be known, we're probably not attracted to each other at all—just caught up in all this romance business, and all mixed-up."

"I'll bet you're right," Mary Kate agreed. Relief washed over her—relief that there was a logical explanation for the way she'd been thinking and acting the past few days. Flynn's wide grin told her he felt the same.

"And now that we've got that settled," he said, reaching to start the engine, "let's get on with this. We've got some business to discuss."

"Do you think we'll be finished by three o'clock?" Mary Kate asked, frowning at her watch. "I'm supposed to have this key I borrowed back by then."

"We'll be done long before that," Flynn assured her as he backed the Jeep out the drive, his face turned toward the outside mirror. "I've already worked out every last detail of this partnership and drawn up the contract. All you have to do is sign on the dotted line—after I explain it to you, of course."

Mary Kate shot the back of his head a hard look. "That's very sweet," she responded through gritted teeth, "but if you don't mind, I think I'd rather *read* it." Then, ever mindful of their fragile peace and determined to keep it, she took several deep breaths, firmly reminding herself that she could put up with anyone—even a die-hard chauvinist—for a chance to live and work in that wonderful old house.

"Whatever you want, honey," Flynn murmured absently, his attention now on his driving.

Mary Kate released her last, calming breath in a slow hiss, letting it serve as an escape valve for her suddenly boiling temper. She ruefully added an "almost" to that "anyone" and then took mental measure of Flynn's handsome neck— a neck she was surely going to wring long before she signed on any dotted line.

Over two hours later, Flynn willed his growling stomach to hush, promising to buy it the biggest steak in town the minute Mary Kate signed the contract—assuming she ever *did*. Never in his life had he dealt with a client so determined to examine every sentence—no, every word. Not that he minded her caution. He didn't really. It indicated a sound head for business: a must in a partner.

Partner? Flynn sighed, wondering if that state of affairs would ever come to be, and how he would survive if it didn't. The idea of Mary Kate working and living in *his* house—the one he'd fantasized about renovating and someday occupying himself—had quickly become an obsession. He could just see her busy behind a counter creating a floral work of art, or slipping into the kitchen for a midnight snack, dressed in whatever lacy nothing she wore to bed.

Flynn smiled wryly at his wayward thoughts, realizing that knowing Mary Kate's cold nature, she probably slept in a flannel granny gown. Suddenly a new vision replaced his earlier one and he imagined how sexy she would look in one of those gowns—or better yet, out of it. He bit back a groan, quickly signaling for a coffee refill.

"Want a warm-up?" he asked Mary Kate when the waitress brought over the steaming pot.

"Hmm?" Mary Kate murmured without looking up from the papers strewed all over the table in front of her.

Flynn sighed, nodding for the waitress to go ahead and fill Mary Kate's cup again.

"Would you like to see a menu?" the woman asked when she finished her task. "We have eight different varieties of waffles and six flavors of syrup."

Taking that as a not-so-subtle hint that the table they had occupied for so long might be worth more than a fifty-cent cup of coffee and half a dozen free refills, Flynn gave up on having his steak. He reached across to tap the back of Mary Kate's hand. "How about a bite to eat?"

The redhead dragged her eyes away from the multipaged contract with obvious difficulty, staring at Flynn blankly for just a moment before she looked back down, saying nothing.

He rolled his eyes heavenward and then grinned at the waitress, who stifled a giggle. "Something tells me we may be here awhile yet, but I'm afraid I've already had my breakfast. What else do you have?"

"Three kinds of cobblers—cherry, peach and apple—and ice cream."

"Did someone say cobbler?" Mary Kate suddenly interjected, turning the last page of the contract over with a decisive flick of her wrist. She picked up the thick stack of papers, meticulously straightening them, and then smiled up at the waitress. "Never could resist cherry cobbler—especially with ice cream on it."

"Then that's what we'll have," Flynn told the waitress with a calm he didn't feel. His knotting stomach told him he wouldn't be able to eat a bite of that confection until he heard Mary Kate's decision on the contract; and depending on what she told him, maybe not even then. He waited until the two of them were alone again before he blurted, "Well, what do you think?"

"I don't know yet," Mary Kate responded, defensively adding, "I have a few questions," after he groaned aloud.

"Ask them."

She did, verbally dissecting each and every clause of the contract that bothered her—and there were several. The arrangement Flynn had put to paper seemed decidedly lopsided to Mary Kate's critical eye, since she would be contributing little but her talent for making things grow until they began to make money, at which point he would get a much larger percentage of the profit. She realized it would take years for Flynn to break even, and couldn't help but wonder at his motives for involving himself in such a venture.

Though Flynn answered satisfactorily each and every question Mary Kate posed to him, her original doubts about her future partner resurfaced. She was thankful when the waitress brought the cobbler, since eating it would give her time to think.

She couldn't help but wonder if Flynn was using this alliance as a means of entangling his life with hers, in spite of all his protestations to the contrary. He'd admitted a "maybe" attraction for her and knew she felt the same. Would she be making the biggest mistake of her life if she signed on that dotted line? Not at all sure of the answer to that, Mary Kate decided there was only one solution to her dilemma.

"How's your cobbler?" she asked the handsome man sitting across from her.

"Fine," he replied, swallowing a bite of it with obvious difficulty. He made a choking sound and threw down his fork. "For God's sake, Mary Kate. We've been here for ages, you've read every word in that damned contract at least twice, and I've answered all your questions. When are you going to sign it?"

"Just as soon as you add an escape clause," she calmly replied.

"What the hell is an 'escape clause'?" he demanded, frowning.

"A few sentences giving me the right to buy out your share of this investment any time I have the cash."

Clearly startled by her request, he hesitated. "You mean you'd pack up, lock, stock and barrel, and move the shop out of my house after all the trouble of renovating it?"

"No. I'd buy it from you," she said. "Assuming you were willing to sell and I could afford it."

Again he hesitated. "I'm not so sure I'd want to sell, but I might rent."

"I could live with that, I guess."

"All right, then. I'll have Carol add your escape clause to the contract as soon as possible and I'll bring it to O'Malley's."

"Not O'Malley's," she said. "My cousin's flower shop in Boulder, The Daisy Patch, on Oak Street. Call before you come and I'll make sure there's someone to cover for me while I read the contract again."

Flynn winced, but didn't comment on that, instead asking, "Now, is there anything else?"

"As a matter of fact, there is," she told him, crossing her arms over her chest and looking him right in the eye. "I want your solemn promise to me that you'll never, ever, call me honey again.''

Those same eyes dancing, Flynn gave her his promise, adding, ''Do you want that in writing?''

''I want it in *blood*.'' That clarified, Mary Kate glanced at her watch, groaning her dismay when she saw the time. "Oh, my gosh, it's after two! That man who loaned me the key said he had another prospective renter wanting to view the place this afternoon. He's going to be hopping mad if I'm late.''

''We won't be late,'' Flynn assured her, leaping to his feet. ''Especially if it'll mean getting that dump of a building safely rented to someone else.'' At that, he scooped up the check and headed to the cashier, pulling out his wallet as he walked.

Mary Kate smiled to herself, highly pleased with the progress they'd made thus far. For the first time in a long while, it seemed very likely that her dreams might come true. Already looking forward to the gargantuan task ahead of her, she gathered up the dog-eared contract and followed him.

Chapter Five

They *did* get the key back to Longmont by three. Then, after a platonic goodbye, Flynn left Mary Kate with a promise that he would be talking to her on Monday. As it turned out, however, a nearly frantic Mary Kate didn't hear from him until late Tuesday afternoon, when he called her at The Daisy Patch as requested.

He got directions to the shop and walked through the glass door in less than an hour after his call, looking so wonderful that Mary Kate's mouth watered. She tried to tell herself that her racing pulse resulted from yesterday's secret doubts that he might have backed out of the partnership, but she knew better. The tingle dancing up her spine had nothing whatsoever to do with business, and neither did her errant desire to feel his mustache tickling her lips.

When Flynn greeted her with that dimpled smile of his, Mary Kate's cousin, standing just behind her, made a strangling sound and dropped the clay pot she held. Mary Kate, fully aware of the impact that expression could have on an unsuspecting female, shot Shannon a look of sympathy and bent down behind the work counter to help pick up the pieces.

"Is that *him*?" Shannon whispered as she snatched up this and that shard of clay.

"That's him."

"Oh, my God." Getting to her feet, Shannon gave Flynn, who now stood just across the counter, her brightest smile. "Hi. I'm Shannon O'Connor, Mary Kate's boss. You must be Flynn Rafferty."

"Yes, I am," he replied with a polite nod, extending his hand. Shannon gave him hers.

"Mary Kate has told me *so* much about you."

"About our *partnership*, you mean," Mary Kate hastily interjected, sending her favorite cousin a killing look.

"Right, right," Shannon murmured absently, taking her hand back with obvious reluctance. She stood in silence then, clearly in a stupor, her eyes glued to the man before her. Mary Kate didn't blame Shannon for staring. Flynn *did* look good enough to eat today—so good she wished she could take a bite. She also wished her cousin wouldn't be quite so obvious. His macho ego didn't need that kind of adoration.

"Well, shall we get down to business?" Mary Kate asked briskly to break the sudden, awkward silence.

"I've got the contract right here," Flynn replied, raising his left hand to show her the leather briefcase he held.

"Good." Mary Kate turned to Shannon, not so gently shaking her arm. "May we use your office?"

"What?" her cousin replied. Then she came to life, obviously getting a grip on herself. "Oh, of course. Use the office. Take as long as you like." She laughed self-consciously, and in a flurry of enthusiasm, hurried to a display shelf to rearrange the flowerpots.

Softly sighing her pity, Mary Kate led the way to the tiny office, motioning for Flynn to follow. Once they were safely inside, she shut the door and grabbed a folding chair, turning it to face the front of Shannon's oak desk. Flynn followed suit, since they needed a place to lay the contract and couldn't possibly look at it together from opposite sides of the massive piece of furniture. Soon they sat knee to knee and almost facing each other while they perused the document he spread out on the table.

"Everything's the same except for the escape clause on this page right here," he told her, flipping to the spot. "But if you want to read it again, I've got plenty of time."

She raised her eyes from the contract, intently studying his expression. Flynn stared right back, unblinking, and Mary Kate, who had to be at O'Malley's in less than half an hour, decided to give him the benefit of the doubt. They were going to be partners, after all. It was time to show a little faith in him.

"I trust you," she said, rewarded for her words by another dazzling smile that she felt clear to the bone. Mary Kate dragged her gaze back to her escape clause with difficulty and then couldn't concentrate on what was typed there. Several minutes and several readings later, she finally reached for an ink pen, signing her name on both copies with a hand that trembled.

Clearly relieved, Flynn then signed his. He heaved a lusty sigh when he'd finished, and tucked his copy of the contract into his briefcase, which he shut with a click of accomplishment. Grinning broadly, he got to his feet, extending his right hand. "Shall we shake on this, partner?"

"Why not?" Mary Kate stood, and they solemnly shook hands to acknowledge their new endeavor. Their gazes locked—a meld of emerald and chocolate. Goose bumps marched down Mary Kate's arms, keeping time to the drumming beat of her heart. Flynn drew a sharp breath and instead of releasing her hand, tugged on it until she took a stumbling step forward, when he wrapped his free arm tightly around her. His gaze dropped to her mouth, which was shamelessly ready and eager to taste his again. Slowly Flynn lowered his head, hesitating only millimeters from a kiss, to stammer, "I don't... We can't..."

Mary Kate solved his dilemma, swiftly closing the remaining distance, pressing her parted lips to his. He opened his mouth in a kiss as intense as the sudden desire that flamed between them and turned slightly, pinning Mary Kate between his body and the desk. Grateful for the support to her jellied knees, she leaned heavily against it. *What are we doing?* her brain screamed, but she hushed it with a *One second more—just one second more, and then never again.* The second grew to several before Flynn lifted his mouth from hers to trail moistly over her cheek, hungrily seeking the highly sensitive flesh just below her ear.

She moaned softly in anticipation, suddenly dead certain that if he kissed her *there* she would lose what remained of her self-control. The realization that she actually wouldn't mind the loss brought Mary Kate abruptly back to her senses.

"We've got to stop," she blurted, terrified at how very badly she wanted Flynn Rafferty. In desperation she wedged her free hand between their molded bodies, pushing him away. He raised his head, expelling a deep breath and inhaling another in an obvious attempt to regain his composure. Then he released her and turned, nervously finger-combing his dark hair with a shaking hand that he really wanted to tangle in Mary Kate's Titian curls. "Damn."

"Damn, too," Mary Kate murmured—a reply that brought a smile to Flynn's lips in spite of himself.

"I guess the time has come to be honest with one another and change Saturday's 'mildly attracted' to *wildly* attracted."

She nodded her agreement, always careful, he noted, to keep her eyes averted from his still-tingling lips—lips he wanted to press to hers again . . . and again.

"And now that we've admitted that, what are we going to do about it?" he then asked, turning his chair away from the desk and collapsing into it.

"Absolutely nothing," she exclaimed, her eyes suddenly cold. "'Mildly' or 'wildly' attracted, I have no intentions of getting involved with you on anything but a professional level. I have so many plans, Flynn—plans that demand independence. I will *not* give them up for a fling that could easily wreck our friendship, our partnership, and our lives. Business and pleasure don't mix. Do you understand what I'm saying?"

"Of course," he told her, pouting just a little, anyway.

"I wonder if you really do," she murmured under her breath, eyeing him with obvious doubt.

"Don't wonder. Believe it." Flynn got to his feet, pacing the room to alleviate some of his agitation. "My business is very important to me, too. I've always been careful to keep my personal life separate from my professional one, and have no plans to change my policy now. This crazy attraction between us is a hell of a nuisance and a threat to our working relationship."

"Then I suggest we make a pact," Mary Kate said, stepping into his path to halt him. "From now on it's strictly business between us."

"Strictly business," he echoed dully. Then he said it again with more conviction, hoping that would soothe the sudden ache in his heart. "Strictly business."

"You swear?" she persisted.

"I swear," he said. "And you?"

"I swear, too."

They stared at each other regretfully for a moment, without speaking. Then Mary Kate turned and walked to the door, putting her hand on the knob. "I have to be at O'Malley's in a few minutes, so if that's all you need . . ."

Flynn took the hint, grasping the handle of his briefcase and joining her there. "I guess you'll be giving him notice now, and your cousin, too."

"Shannon has already been warned," Mary Kate told him, sidestepping the issue of O'Malley's. Once before, Flynn had hinted that she would want to quit working there, but she had no intention of doing such a thing. The events of this afternoon had given her serious doubts about the success of her partnership with him. She needed the job at O'Malley's to ensure some sort of fiscal independence in case everything fell through.

Flynn didn't seem to notice her ploy and, after giving her a ghost of a smile that showed he might be just a little concerned about future relations himself, turned to head back across the shop. Before he reached the door, however, he pivoted, returning to Mary Kate, who now stood by the cash register with Shannon.

"I almost forgot," he said, propping his briefcase on the counter and then shuffling through the papers inside it until he grunted in satisfaction, producing an old-fashioned house key, the kind that looked as if it might open a treasure box somewhere. He handed it to her with a grin. "It's all yours now, hon—uh, Mary Kate, but I suggest you clean up the place a little before you move in. There might be rats or spiders or—"

"I get the picture," Mary Kate responded wryly, thinking that that wasn't at all the kind of treasure she planned to unlock.

"Should we hire someone to help you?" Flynn then asked, frowning slightly. "The place is structurally sound, of course, and the third floor is probably in the best shape of any of them since it's such a climb up there, but you still might need help—"

"No help," Mary Kate told him. "Remember what we decided—that I'd clean and decorate that floor just enough to make it livable. It'll be fine until after the shop is all done and we're making a little cash. Then we'll talk about major renovation."

Though clearly tempted to argue, Flynn didn't. Instead he nodded his agreement, turned on his heel and walked back across the shop. Halfway there, he began to whistle, slightly off-key, a tune that Mary Kate immediately recognized as "My Wild Irish Rose."

She waited until the glass door shut behind him and then turned to hug Shannon, squealing her pent-up delight. "It's going to happen. It's really going to happen. My own shop. *I can't believe it!*"

Shannon hugged her back, laughing. "So, what are you going to call this shop of yours?"

Mary Kate hesitated only a second before she turned to gaze thoughtfully toward the door through which Flynn had just disappeared. She smiled slightly, nodded decisively and replied, "How does My Wild Irish Rose grab you?"

"Perfect," Shannon pronounced. "Just perfect."

The next days were killers for Mary Kate. She got up at the crack of dawn and drove to Denver—not always an easy feat, since winter was in full swing and frequent snowfalls were a fact of life. She never ate breakfast and seldom ate lunch, hating to lose precious minutes she needed to devote to cleaning "her" beautiful old house.

And what a house it was—an extravagant mixture of classical styles, characterized by spacious hallways, wide staircases and rambling rooms. Mary Kate, who easily envisioned how the structure might have looked at one time, immediately fell in love with every dusty, dirty, cluttered inch of it. Though sorely tempted to begin work on the first floor, which was the area visitors would see upon entering the house, she stuck to the third floor, her future home.

That floor consisted of two "attic" bedrooms, both quite spacious in spite of the slanted ceilings, and a bath, which had most likely been added in the 1900s and sported a footed tub. Mary Kate decided to use one bedroom as an office and saved the cleaning of it for the last, since her goal was to get moved from Boulder as quickly as possible.

She had no qualms about moving to Denver other than the fact that she would now be traveling the highway between the two cities when she got off at O'Malley's, usually after midnight. Though a less-than-ideal situation, it was one Mary Kate could and would handle and without letting Flynn know what was going on. She knew he would only deliver one of his famous you-haven't-got-a-lick-of-sense lectures, and being very determined to retain her independence, she didn't intend to listen to it.

On Monday, Mary Kate filled several trash bags with the junk of many years' accumulation and hauled each down the two flights of stairs so she could vacuum and dust until her eyes watered and her head ached. That massive chore took all day, but she looked with pride on the empty rooms before she headed back to Boulder and O'Malley's.

On Tuesday she scrubbed the fireplace and disinfected the bathroom until her hands were so chapped, no amount of lotion would save them. By late afternoon Mary Kate's labors paid off, and as planned, she indulged herself, soaking for a few minutes in that marvelous, if slightly chipped, tub in her almost presentable bathroom. Then she changed into the shiny green uniform she'd brought with her and hit the road again.

Wednesday, at four in the morning—her usual rising hour these busy days—Mary Kate grimaced at the exhausted young woman who peered back at her from the bathroom mirror in her Boulder apartment. Dark circles of weariness had appeared under her bloodshot eyes almost overnight— a sure sign it was time to slow down just a tad. But she didn't dare do that—not if she wanted to get out of her apartment without paying another month's rent on it.

Midafternoon that same day, Flynn made a surprise visit to the house, opening the door and shouting up the stairs to let her know she had company.

"Come on in," Mary Kate called to him before scurrying to the bathroom to try to make herself presentable. She didn't even give the why of that sudden attack of vanity a moment's thought, too worried with trying to see her face in the aged mirror mounted on the wall. Most of the silver backing had peeled away through the years, leaving just about two square inches of functional reflecting surface. Snorting her exasperation, Mary Kate gave up and dashed back to the stairs, impatiently snatching up the broom that lay in her path. Calmly she greeted a huffing and puffing Flynn when he stepped into the wide hallway at the top of the staircase.

"Quite a climb, huh?" she teased, oh-so-happy to see him again.

"Damn" was all he said before he sank down on the first step to catch his breath. "I guess I'm not in as good a shape as I thought."

Oh, but you are, Mary Kate silently argued, letting her hungry eyes feast on his long legs and broad shoulders, set off to perfection by dark pants and a herringbone sport jacket in muted heather tones. She glanced down at her own attire and grimaced. Her oversize sweatshirt, handed down from a brother, had certainly seen better days, as had the faded jeans that sported a gaping hole in the left knee. Pink bunny slippers completed the outfit—an addition not missed by Flynn, who, she realized, was making a sweeping inspection of his own. He grinned when he saw them, but said nothing, instead pulling himself back to his feet.

"Making any progress?" he asked.

"Just wait till you see," she replied, capturing his wrist to drag him—and her broom—to the bedroom. He halted in the doorway, perusing the area. Mary Kate tried to see it through his eyes but found she couldn't. She had long since lost her perspective and fallen in love with this room, which was very much a part of her now.

Flynn turned to her, his expressive eyes wide with astonishment. "When did you start on this?"

"Monday. Why?"

"My God, Mary Kate," he exclaimed, stepping through the door. "You've worked a miracle! I can't believe it." He turned slowly, his eyes sweeping the clean walls, the freshly hung drapes, the shampooed carpet. "You must get up with the chickens and go to bed with the owls."

Mary Kate could only agree, since that's exactly how she'd managed her 'miracle.' "You've got that right," she murmured.

Some of her exhaustion must have been revealed in her words, for Flynn turned his attention to her face, studying it through eyes narrowed in suspicion. "Just what time *do* you get here in the mornings?"

She shrugged, not meeting that intense stare. "Pretty early."

"How early?"

"Around five-ish."

He digested that in silence and then said, "I see. And what time do you get back to bed?"

Thankful he'd phrased his question just that way, Mary Kate murmured, "Pretty late."

"How late?" he demanded, in a little louder voice. He'd stepped forward now and cupped her chin with his fingers, raising her face to catch the afternoon sunlight that streamed through the floor-to-ceiling windows. He brushed his thumb over the dark smudges under her eyes, as if to verify that they were real, and swore softly under his breath, harshly repeating, "How damn late?"

"One-thirty or so," she blurted defensively, twisting away.

"Hell fire, Mary Kate!" Flynn exploded. "Are you trying to kill yourself?"

"No, of course not. I—"

"When do you eat?"

"When I get hungry," she retorted, but again she couldn't look him in the eye.

"What have you had today?"

"Uh . . . I had some cookies around noon and half a cola—"

"Damn." He came to life, snatching the broom from her hand and tossing it into a corner with a clatter. Then he reached for Mary Kate, grabbing her wrist and dragging her toward the door. "Come on."

She struggled to keep her feet, demanding, "Where are we going?"

"To get the breakfast, lunch and dinner you skipped, that's where," he stormed, striding purposefully to the stairs.

Mary Kate dug her heels into the carpet, resisting until he halted his trek and turned to confront her, his mouth a grim line of concern. "I can't," she told him.

"Why not?"

"I—" she took a deep breath and squared her shoulders, knowing she couldn't hide the truth from him forever "—I have to be at O'Malley's in an hour."

Stunned silence followed her confession. Flynn dropped her hand and stared at her, opening his mouth as though he wanted to speak but couldn't find words. Mary Kate gulped and took a step back, sensing he was surely about to explode and not wanting to get caught by the shrapnel.

A wise move, that, because Flynn *did* blow up, yelling exactly what he thought of foolish young women who worked two jobs when one would do fine. His tirade, liberally sprinkled with every expletive she'd ever heard and a few she hadn't, also included picturesque comments about her Irish stubbornness, her alarming "suicidal" tendencies and, of all things, sympathy for her big brothers.

Mary Kate choked at that, but held her peace until Flynn paused for air. Then she vented her fury at him, shouting in no uncertain terms exactly what he could do with his unwanted advice and punctuating every word with a forefinger jabbed into his broad chest.

"And furthermore," she finally exclaimed, several loud moments later, "my days may be half yours, Flynn Rafferty, but my nights are mine—and always will be."

"You're killing yourself," he roared.

"That's my privilege," she screamed back. Then, both of them winded and panting, they stood in blessed silence, face-to-face and glaring at each other.

"I'm going to call O'Malley right now and tell him you're quitting," Flynn said after a moment, his voice much calmer. He turned deliberately toward the stairs.

"You do, and I'm out of here," Mary Kate warned, her voice just as steady. Flynn stopped short and whirled to confront her. He scrutinized her face, obviously gauging her sincerity.

"You'd do it, wouldn't you?"

"I would, and I will, if you don't back off. You have no right to tell me what to do. I'm a grown woman with a mind of my own—a darned *intelligent* mind of my own, I might add."

"That's surely a matter of opinion," he retorted, immediately qualifying that with "I didn't really mean that. You *are* an intelligent woman—too intelligent to do this to yourself. That's why I'm sure if you give this thing a little thought, you'll give notice at the pub tonight.''

"I'll give notice when I'm good and ready—and not a moment before,'' she said, coldly adding, "Now, if you'll excuse me, I'm going to take a quick bath and get out of here. O'Malley's awaits me.''

With that, she stepped around Flynn and stalked to the bathroom, which she entered, shutting and locking the door behind her. She didn't start her bath at once, but stood, ear to the door, listening for the creak of the stairs, which would tell her that Flynn had gone.

She heard those telltale boards as expected, and waited several minutes longer before she crept out of the bathroom and down the stairs to see if he was gone. A quick peek out the small window beside the front door assured her there was no Jeep parked in the drive. Only then did Mary Kate exhale a sigh of relief and trudge back up the stairs to the haven of a bath.

Mary Kate didn't see or hear from Flynn again that week—a development she viewed with mixed emotions. On the one hand, it was good to know he'd taken seriously her threat to dissolve the partnership if he didn't butt out; but on the other, she missed him. The terrifying part of this realization was that Flynn, who was so very much like her father and her brothers, had already finagled a part of her heart.

What a bossy man! And how manipulative! His actions told her that he was used to submission from the women in his life, and Mary Kate had no intention of taking her place in those ranks—even if she never saw him again.

Friday night at ten found Mary Kate back at O'Malley's—overworked and irritable. She glanced longingly toward the pub exit at a few minutes past the hour, blinking in surprise when Jessie and Tex chose that moment to walk through it. With a gasp of delight, Mary Kate wound her way through the tables and the boisterous Friday-night crowd to hug the friend she hadn't seen in two weeks. Mere yards away from the waving pair, however, she found her path blocked by the denim-clad leg of an inebriated cowboy.

"What's your hurry, little lady?" he asked, getting to his feet to tower over her.

Why me? Mary Kate thought, slowly raising her gaze to his and forcing the smile that on any other night would have come naturally. Famous in the pub for her ability to tactfully put any amorous male in his place, Mary Kate always had a smooth comeback. But not tonight, apparently. Bone weary, all she wanted to do was give him a swift one-two that would take care of his loud mouth once and for all.

But she didn't, of course. "I was just going to say hello to a couple of friends I haven't seen for a while," Mary Kate explained, stepping to the right and trying to ease around him. But once more, he blocked her path.

"Forget them. I'll be your friend tonight." He raised a hand, tugging a lock of her russet hair—a move that made Mary Kate's stomach turn.

Still she kept her cool. "How about another beer?"

"I want something besides beer from you."

"I'm afraid beer is all I'm offering." Her voice had a definite edge to it now—one that might have been warning enough to a sober man. Unfortunately this cowboy was far past sober and a borderline idiot.

"Aw, come on, honey," he drawled, sliding his fingertips down her bare arm. "The night's young. We could slip out back...."

Honey. A simple word, that, but one Mary Kate despised, probably since it was flung at her at least fifty times every night. She usually tuned it out—except in Flynn's case, of course, when she'd found it intolerable. But tonight she couldn't. She'd dealt with more than her fair share of arrogant males in the past few days. And this one had added insult to injury by touching her. She didn't have to put up with that kind of harassment—even here.

"Don't call me 'honey' and if you *ever* lay a finger on me again, you're dead meat. Got it?"

The cowboy started at those words, which Mary Kate suspected she'd uttered a shade louder than she intended to. The raucous laughter of his companions at the table confirmed her suspicions. "Looks like you're going to owe me that bill after all, Clint," one of them called out.

So they'd had a bet. Suddenly wishing she'd let him down just a little easier, Mary Kate raised her eyes to the man in front of her. She flinched and took an involuntary step back from the cold fury she saw in his eyes before sidestepping him, this time successfully, to make tracks to the table where Jessie and Tex had seated themselves, clear across the room. Halfway to that table, she stumbled to a halt, suddenly realizing the two of them were no longer alone.

Flynn had joined them—Flynn, looking marvelous in cords and a sweater. Disgustingly affected by the sight of him, she hesitated, trying to regroup before she continued on. His eyes met hers across the room and she saw a steely glint of anger there. Is he still upset with me? she wondered briefly, before he shifted his gaze to a point somewhere behind her. Realizing he'd no doubt witnessed that little run-in moments ago and already had his I-told-you-so lecture prepared, Mary Kate toyed with the idea of escaping to the safety of the kitchen.

The idea had only momentary appeal. It would be a hot day in January before she let the likes of him intimidate her. Steadfastly she continued on, arriving at the table mere moments later, to find herself engulfed in Jessie's comforting embrace.

"Are you okay?" the brunette asked, frowning worriedly at her.

"I'm fine." Mary Kate replied. "And awfully glad you're here. O'Malley's just hasn't been the same without you." She turned to Tex, greeting him with a smile. "How's married life?"

"Perfect," he told her, adding, "Which just goes to show that you two jokers don't know everything." He pointed toward Flynn when he spoke—a gesture that naturally included the Irishman in their circle of friendship.

Mary Kate swallowed convulsively, greeting her dark-eyed partner with a brief "Hi, Flynn."

He didn't speak, acknowledging her presence with nothing more than a cool nod. Deliberately, Mary Kate turned her back on him, a move that caused Jessie and Tex to exchange a puzzled frown.

Intercepting that frown, Mary Kate realized that Flynn must have kept their latest altercation to himself—a state of affairs that suited her just fine. It would have been difficult explaining her feelings about Flynn and this partnership to Jessie when she didn't understand them herself.

"What are you guys drinking tonight?" Mary Kate asked, swiftly smoothing over an awkward moment. In minutes she was back at work, taking orders, making small talk, pocketing tips. She stopped to say a few words to Jessie every chance she could—not an easy task since it was standing room only and everyone seemed to be thirsty.

At five minutes to midnight Tex and Jessie said their goodbyes, wanting to avoid the closing-time traffic. Flynn left when they did, without uttering a word, which didn't really surprise Mary Kate even if it did hurt her feelings just a little.

Sure, they'd argued. But with both their Irish temperaments and her red hair, that was to be expected, after all. Was this what she could anticipate every time they didn't agree personally or professionally—hard looks, cold shoulders? If so, this partnership might not be at all what she wanted.

You're just tired. Mary Kate told herself when she realized the negative turn her usually sunny thoughts had made. *Everything will look better tomorrow.*

She glanced at the clock then, suddenly realizing it was tomorrow and past time to leave. All she had to do was get her paycheck from O'Malley. There had been a mistake on it when he handed it to her earlier that evening, and he'd promised to write her another.

He did, a procedure that took several minutes since he wasn't much of a bookkeeper. Finally, check in hand, Mary Kate made her way to the door, grateful that most of her co-workers were long gone and she wouldn't have to make any more small talk. She'd had just about all she could handle that day.

Mary Kate didn't bother with her usual wrap-up ritual or her boots, choosing instead to take the faster way out and make do with nothing more than her jacket. She stepped outside the pub, noting that, for once, it hadn't snowed, though a chilling wind had risen. Ever mindful of hidden patches of ice, she headed across the lot to her car, which was parked in a shadowy section reserved for employees. Just as she reached it she heard the crunch of a heavy footfall just behind her.

Unperturbed, Mary Kate glanced automatically over her shoulder, ready to make a polite comment about the weather to one of her co-workers. But it wasn't a fellow employee who followed; it was Clint, the drunken cowboy.

Stay cool, she told herself, increasing her walk to a trot that nearly felled her when she stepped into a tire rut. Clutching at the side of a minivan parked nearby, Mary Kate regained her balance. Then, angry for having been put in the position of prey, she whirled to confront her assailant, who was now less than a yard behind her.

"What do you want?" she asked, straightening to her full height.

"What do you think?" he snarled, taking a menacing step forward. Mary Kate took a matching step back, a thoughtless move that put the van between her and the pub—exactly what the cowboy had intended. He took another step toward her.

"Beat it," she said, abruptly realizing they were now hidden from view. She gauged her possibilities for escape, acknowledging they weren't too good since the snowy lot wouldn't provide much traction for her dress pumps.

"Not yet," he told her, reaching out to capture her wrist. "I just lost a hundred bucks because of you, and I intend to get it back—with interest."

"Just try it," a very familiar voice suddenly warned. Not quite believing her ears, Mary Kate craned her neck to see around Clint and sagged with relief when Flynn stepped out from behind the van.

Clint stiffened, abruptly releasing Mary Kate to whirl and face this unexpected adversary. "Who the hell are you?" he demanded.

"Get in the car, Mary Kate," Flynn said instead of answering, his voice deadly calm.

"But I—"

"Do it!"

She did, scrambling to get into her station wagon. Once there, she rolled her window down a scant inch, determined to hear what transpired, even if she couldn't have a hand in it. To her disgust, however, Flynn stepped between the cowboy and her car, successfully blocking her view. She then heard the murmur of a muted conversation, but couldn't make out a single word—a fact that only served to frustrate her further.

Seconds later, Clint walked over to the car where she sat and tipped his hat, muttering "My apologies, ma'am," before he slithered off into the night.

Mary Kate leaped from the car and skated around it, grabbing the sleeve of his sweater and demanding, "What'd you say to him?"

"Never mind that," Flynn snapped. "I want to know why you didn't park closer to the pub."

"This is the employees' section," she countered. "And I've never had any trouble here before tonight."

He didn't respond, turning on his heel to stalk to his Jeep, parked a few yards away.

Suddenly remorseful that she hadn't even thanked him for coming to her rescue, Mary Kate called, "Flynn! Wait!"

He halted without turning, waiting for her to make her way over to him.

"Thanks for your help. I don't know what I'd have done if—"

Her last words were smothered against Flynn's thudding heart. Wrapped suddenly in his strong arms, Mary Kate fought the tears that sprang from nowhere—hot tears of uncertainty, fear and exhaustion. She hugged him back, hiding her face in the scratchy wool of his sweater until she could get control of herself again—not an easy feat in the face of his sympathy and concern.

"Are you all right?" he asked, his voice husky-soft.

"Yes."

"I'm going to follow you home."

She raised her head then, blinking hastily, determined not to reveal her weakness. "There's no need."

"I'm going to follow you home," he repeated. "I want to be sure you're okay."

His tone indicated he would brook no argument, so Mary Kate hastily relented, telling herself it was because she wanted to find out what he'd said to Clint, and not because she needed him—not at all.

Chapter Six

When they arrived at Mary Kate's apartment, Flynn parked his Jeep in the drive behind her car and followed her inside the house. She motioned him to the living room, but made a beeline to the bedroom herself, dying to get into warmer clothes. One Kelly green sweat suit and a pair of argyle knee socks later, she joined Flynn on the couch where he sat, solemn as a wooden Indian.

"Can I get you something?" she asked. "Coffee? Tea? Cola?"

"You're off duty now," he responded, getting to his feet and surprising them both by suggesting, "Why don't I get *you* something instead?"

Mary Kate never even pretended to argue, instead sinking back into the mauve corduroy couch, closing her eyes and pointing to the kitchen. "Anything wet."

Smiling to himself, Flynn stepped around a potted plant and walked into the kitchen dining-room combination, flicking on the overhead light to make himself at home. He looked first in her refrigerator, curiously perusing the contents. There he found yogurt, salad makings, diet soft drinks, low-fat milk and little else.

No wonder she's so trim, he thought, quickly banishing that thought since it brought to mind how nice that "trim" body felt pressed to his. Such visions would only hinder his ability to think, and he needed all his faculties if he intended to sweet-talk her into quitting O'Malley's. And he *was* going to do that.

Whistling, Flynn then inspected the cupboard. It was in no better shape, yielding a few canned vegetables, some chicken-noodle soup, and tuna. Suddenly inspired, he retrieved the tuna before he turned back to the refrigerator to get mayonnaise, a couple of eggs, and dill pickles.

In minutes the eggs were boiling in a saucepan on the gas range and the tuna, mayonnaise and pickles were stirred together, awaiting their addition. While the eggs cooked, Flynn walked around the tiny room, done up in sunshine yellow and sapphire blue. He decided the place had Mary Kate's mark on it, from the unusual ceramic canisters decorating the counter, to the plants that occupied every nook, cranny and windowsill.

Never one to pay much attention to foliage, himself, Flynn stood in awe of the many varieties of greenery scattered about. The plants ranged in size from dainty to huge, in color from the usual green to a deep reddish-purple. The one plant he did recognize, a shamrock, was a credit to its species—just like the one in his office these days. Flynn remembered that Mary Kate talked to her plants, and acknowledged that this method of "fertilization" obviously worked.

Then, wondering why she wasn't talking to *him,* he walked over to the door and peered out into the living room, shaking his head ruefully when he discovered Mary Kate had curled up on the sofa and fallen asleep. He stared at her in silence for a moment, relishing the sight of her tousled hair, which he knew felt as soft as silk, and her full lips, slightly parted and so kissably soft. What a beauty! He wanted to hold her, touch her. He wanted to cherish her . . . forever.

Forever? *Get a grip!* Flynn told himself, pivoting to stalk back to the stove. He didn't want forever from Mary Kate. He didn't want it from any woman. It was time he got that straight, once and for all.

So why am I fixing her dinner? he wondered, brows knitted in a worried frown as he fumbled for an explanation for his uncharacteristic generosity. Telling himself the meal was nothing more than a bribe—a means of getting on her good side so he could win their latest battle—Flynn deliberately turned his attention to the eggs, which were now ready to add to the tuna. That accomplished, he toasted some of the bread he found in the bread box and built them both a sandwich. Then he poured two glasses of milk. Balancing all this on a pizza pan—he couldn't locate a tray—he walked into the living room and set it on the coffee table, next to yet another plant.

Though he hated to waken Mary Kate, he nonetheless did, dead certain she hadn't eaten all day. She stirred with a kittenlike purr that did amazing things to his blood pressure, and sat up, stretching lazily. Resisting an intense urge to coax her back down on the couch and to join her there, Flynn thrust the "tray" in her direction.

Mary Kate stared at it, clearly startled, and burst into tears. Flynn gaped at her in horror and then came to life, snatching back the food. "You don't have to eat it."

"B-but I want to," she sobbed, burying her face in her hands.

Suddenly realizing that her uncharacteristic display of emotion no doubt resulted from fear and exhaustion and not from his feeble attempts to cook, Flynn abandoned the tray and joined her on the couch. He lay an arm gingerly across her shoulders, awkwardly patting her—a show of sympathy that only served to make her cry harder.

"Oh, what the hell," he then muttered, tossing caution out the window to the winter winds. He wrapped both arms around her in a full-fledged embrace that he would surely rue later on when it was just a haunting memory—if not before. Mary Kate turned automatically into the curve of his body, accepting the comfort he gave, her face pressed into the patch of sweater just over his heart—a heart now thudding erratically against his rib cage. Exerting willpower he didn't know he possessed, Flynn didn't kiss her or even tangle his fingers in her russet curls. Instead he held her in silence, waiting for her sobs to die away. Then, when her tears were no more than an occasional sniffle—a sound he could barely hear over the jackhammering of his heart—he cleared his throat and murmured, "Are you asleep?"

"No." Willing her languid muscles back to life, Mary Kate eased free of Flynn, self-consciously swiping at her still-damp cheeks. "Sorry about that. I don't know what's wrong with me."

"I do. You've worked yourself to exhaustion this week," Flynn told her, shifting at least a foot away from her on the couch. "And that brings to mind the next topic of conversation: your job at O'Malley's."

"I've said all I have to say on the subject," Mary Kate responded firmly, brushing away one last stray tear.

"Good," he replied, handing her the sandwich and the milk again. "*I'll* do the talking. You eat." Mary Kate watched in amazement as he got to his feet and began to prowl the room, hands clasped behind his back, brow furrowed in thought. Finally he stopped right in front of her and said, "As you recall, our contract made stipulations for your living expenses beginning the moment you started renovating the house and ending when the shop became solvent, at which point you'd receive a straight percentage of the profit. Am I right?''

"You know you are," Mary Kate barely managed to mumble around a huge bite of sandwich.

"I believe you agreed that the arrangement was fair."

"That's what I agreed, yes."

"Then would you please explain why you're risking life and limb, not to mention your health, by working at a bar until the wee hours of the morning?'' Flynn raged.

"Lower your voice," she warned. "I have neighbors who are trying to sleep."

Flynn took a deep breath and leaned down to plant his hands on either side of Mary Kate's legs on the couch. Then, with his mustache against her ear, he whispered, "Why are you still at O'Malley's?"

"Because I'm too old to get an allowance," she retorted, pushing him away.

"Damn it, Mary Kate!" he exploded, straightening up and throwing his hands into the air. "I'm not giving you an allowance. You've slaved in that house from dawn till dusk every day this week. Don't you think you've earned every penny you get from me?''

"Shh," she whispered, a second later adding, "Of course I've earned *something*, but it galls me to have to account for every lipstick or loaf of bread I choose to buy. I may as well be married and stuck at home playing housewife."

"Oh, for—" He shook his head in disbelief, clearly struggling for patience. "It's only for a few months."

"A few months too long," she retorted. "I can't live like that. I have to maintain some fiscal independence."

"Why didn't you say something earlier—when we were hashing this whole arrangement out?"

She shrugged. "Because it wasn't an issue since I'd planned to stay on at O'Malley's and have plenty of spending money."

He stood in silence for a moment, obviously considering her words. "All right, then. Work another job if you must. Just do me a favor and find someplace else to do it—a safer place."

"O'Malley's usually *is* safe," she said. "And that reminds me. What did you say to that jerk a while ago to make him apologize like that?"

"That doesn't matter. What *does* matter is that you nearly got yourself hurt tonight and it could easily happen again. That's why I think you should change jobs. Surely we can come up with *something* you'll like."

Mary Kate, busy polishing off the last of her sandwich, didn't reply at once. That done, she pointed to Flynn's portion, which lay untouched on the pizza pan. "Are you going to eat that?"

He shook his head.

"Mind if I . . . ?"

"Help yourself."

Ignoring the amusement in his voice, she did. After taking another big bite, she said, "I'm open to suggestions—" prompting when he frowned "—about my new night job."

Flynn's face lit up. "Right, right. Your new night job." He began to pace again, thinking aloud with each step. "Let's see. . . . You could always work in one of those convenience stores sprinkled all over town—the ones that get robbed two or three times a week."

"That ought to be safer than O'Malley's," Mary Kate dryly agreed.

"Or you could wait tables at that all-night greasy spoon out on the freeway," Flynn went on without blinking an eye. "I believe it comes highly recommended among escaped convicts and hitchhikers."

"Oh. Better still."

"*Or* you could work the check-in desk at the Stolen Moments Motel. First-class establishment, that. Why, all the best—and loneliest—traveling salesmen stay there. You'd be welcomed with open arms . . . literally.''

Mary Kate nearly choked on her milk. "Any more bright ideas?" she asked with difficulty, trying to contain the laughter threatening to bubble forth.

"Fresh out," Flynn admitted. "Have you got one?"

"Maybe," she murmured, tilting her head to study his earnest expression. Flynn's antics in the last little while—from the surprise supper to his blatant concern for her safety—had caught her unawares, warmed her to him. And though Mary Kate knew she could blame mental and physical exhaustion for this dangerous susceptibility, she found herself helpless to resist his killer smile and pleading brown eyes. "I heard there's a guy in Denver—an investor—who's looking for someone to renovate his house and put a flower shop in it. I might consider that position on a full-time basis if he'd pay a salary instead of living expenses."

"That would make the difference even though the amount would probably be about the same?"

"Yes."

"Hmm," Flynn murmured, rubbing his chin thoughtfully. Mary Kate noted that his eyes had begun to twinkle. "Sounds damned fishy to me. Are you sure you can trust this joker?"

"Of course, I'm sure. He's Irish. Besides, if I took that job, I could give up O'Malley's."

"You could?"

"I could."

"And you *would*?"

She nodded, giving in once and for all. "I would."

"When?" he pressed.

"Tomorrow? I want to do it in person since I won't be giving any notice."

"Hot damn!" Smiling broadly, Flynn reached for his milk, as yet untouched, and raised the glass to Mary Kate.

"To the luck of the Irish that started this partnership and somehow keeps it alive."

"To the luck," Mary Kate agreed with a smile that turned into a yawn she didn't even try to hide.

Flynn downed his drink in one long gulp and set the empty glass on the table. "I think that's my cue to get lost. Will you be okay now?"

"I'll be fine," she assured him, getting to her feet. When Flynn began to stack plates and glasses on the tray she waved a hand at him. "Leave it, leave it. I'll clean up—" she yawned again "—tomorrow."

Chuckling, Flynn complied. He took a step toward Mary Kate, placing a quick kiss—all he dared allow himself—on her forehead before he strode out the door and into the black of night. Only when he heard her apartment door shut behind him did he raise his fists starward in jubilant celebration of this latest victory in their ongoing battle of wills.

He thought back to similar battles he'd won in his life— hard-fought battles with his younger sister, Peg, who was every bit as bullheaded as Mary Kate and certain she knew what was best for *her* life, too. Those battles were excellent preparation for this partnership, and Flynn credited tonight's relatively easy manipulation of Mary Kate to his years of practice with Peg. Still deep in mental self-congratulation, he got into his Jeep and started it.

Mary Kate heard the powerful engine from behind her front door where she still stood, frowning slightly. A little disappointed by Flynn's brotherly peck, she mentally replayed the past hour of her life, beginning with the minute he stepped inside her apartment and ending when he walked out of it.

They'd shared a hug, engaged in a rational discussion, and parted on friendly terms—an astonishing development and one that left her with an oddly bewildered feeling. Why? she wondered. Wasn't that the way business partners were supposed to behave? And wasn't that the only type of relationship she could handle with Flynn at this point in her life—even if she'd half expected a pass and probably would have welcomed it?

Of course, she acknowledged, heading for her bedroom and the granny gown in which she always slept. Mere moments later found her burrowed under flannel sheets and a stack of homemade quilts, wiggling her toes to help them warm up to the 98.6 degrees the rest of her body now enjoyed. Drowsy and hovering on the brink of sleep, she let her mind wander at will. Not surprisingly, a forbidden fantasy formed itself in her head—a fantasy of her handsome Irishman stretched out beside her on the bed. Sinfully handsome, deliciously warm, he held her and kissed her until she was putty to his touch.

Putty to his touch? Wide-awake now, Mary Kate sat bolt upright in bed, seeing the events of the last hour from a totally different perspective. Why did he make that sandwich? she wondered. Why all that sympathy? That irresistible comedy routine?

"He did it on purpose to confuse me," she groaned, slapping her flattened palm to her forehead. "And it worked. I actually let him talk me out of O'Malley's. What an idiot I am!" Clearly the man was dangerous—no, lethal—as skilled in getting what he wanted as her father and brothers. She felt like a puppet dangling on a string, waiting for his next command. Thank goodness he hadn't made a pass tonight, after all....

Mary Kate groaned again, flopping back on the bed, arms outflung. Had Flynn omitted a more passionate good-night kiss on purpose, just to keep her off balance and aching for him? Was this whole evening part of some diabolical plot to distract her from her carefully set career goals, to make her a prisoner of her heart?

"Never again," Mary Kate vowed. "I'm going to keep my head. Business partners we are and business partners we remain!"

She talked to that "business partner" only briefly on Saturday, when he verified that she really wouldn't be returning to O'Malley's and would be moving to Denver that weekend. He vetoed her plan to rent a U-Haul and get the pub's bouncer—an oversize male with a very strong back— to help her. Flynn told her that a business acquaintance of his, the owner of a furniture store, had agreed to loan them his delivery truck for the day. He assured her that *his* strong back was the only one she would need, and since her Boulder apartment had come furnished, she gave in to him. What few pieces Mary Kate did have were antiques and she didn't intend to entrust their welfare and that of her precious plants to a stranger. Besides, why rent a truck when she could borrow one?

Flynn backed said truck into her driveway at eight on Sunday morning. Mary Kate, dressed for the weather in a bulky sweater, corduroy jeans, and boots, met him on the porch. She turned her back to the chilly wind and looked up, noting with disgust the charcoal-gray skies now spitting snow and threatening worse. Mary Kate sent heavenward a little prayer that the major snowstorm in the weather forecast would hold off a few hours longer—at least until she was safe in that marvelous house of Flynn's, which had a fireplace in almost every room.

She tried to be nothing more than coolly cordial to her dark-haired companion—not an easy task since her heart turned over at the mere sight of him. And what a sight— aged leather aviator jacket, stone-washed jeans, rakish smile. The man was irresistible dressed like that; but then, she reminded herself sternly, he would be irresistible dressed in nothing.

Flustered by that wayward thought, Mary Kate deliberately turned her face to the cutting wind, hoping to cool her flaming cheeks and matching libido. She glanced back at Flynn, who looked better with every step he took in her direction, and she sagged weakly against the door, wondering if she were really up to what this day might hold.

He greeted her with a grin and a bag of doughnuts, which they quickly consumed over the coffee left in her pot. Then, while he disassembled her bed, the single largest piece of furniture she owned and certainly the most difficult to move, she rinsed out the coffee maker, tucking it away in one of the boxes she'd collected and packed the day before.

Once Flynn had the bed broken down, Mary Kate helped him maneuver the double mattress and box spring out of the apartment and into the truck, via a ramp that bridged front porch to rear fender. The four-poster head and footboards, though solid rosewood, were much easier to manage and soon joined the mattresses. After that, they loaded the matching chest, portable television, stereo and bentwood rocker.

The boxes came next—cartons of every shape and size, filled to capacity with the rest of Mary Kate's worldly goods, everything from her clothes to her junior high-school scrapbook. Though tempted to stop long enough to dig into one of those treasure boxes that would surely reveal Mary Kate's innermost secrets, Flynn controlled himself. He suspected he would just get his hand slapped for his curiosity.

Finally, some two and a half hours later, Flynn lowered the door on the truck. Mary Kate, who'd just completed a last-minute inspection of her apartment, joined him on the porch in time to help him secure it.

"I'm going to take this key to the super, and then I'll follow you to Denver," she told him.

Flynn frowned at her station wagon, which was packed from floor to ceiling with greenery. "Are you sure you'll be able to see out of that thing?"

"Sure I'm sure," she retorted, already headed to the apartment superintendent's office. "Besides, it'll be good practice for when I open my shop and make deliveries."

Determined not to do anything to spoil the easy camaraderie between them, Flynn kept to himself his plans to buy a van for her flower shop as soon as he could talk her into it. That he could talk her into it, he never doubted for a moment. Last night's easy victory had convinced him he had her number. He fully expected this partnership to go his way from now on.

Ten minutes later they were two miles down the highway, headed to Denver. It had begun to snow in earnest, a development Flynn didn't mind in the least, though he suspected Mary Kate well might. He thought of the firewood he'd had delivered to the mansion the day before and reminded himself to teach Mary Kate the finer nuances of lighting a good fire. She was definitely going to need that skill until he decided on which central heating system to purchase—not an easy decision due to the size and age of the house; not to mention its lack of adequate insulation. Meanwhile he'd bought an electric space heater for the bathroom, the only area with no access to a heat source of any kind.

Getting the truck unloaded took the remains of the morning. By the time Flynn had succeeded in manhandling the mattress and box spring up all those stairs, he fervently wished he'd let Mary Kate bring the bouncer along, after all. Luckily she was stronger than she looked and a lot of help to him. Their efforts paid off, and just after four o'clock they finished their task, collapsing onto the carpeted floor, both gasping for air and aching all over.

"We're going to pay for this tomorrow, you know," Mary Kate warned, turning over on her side to get a better look at the man stretched out full length not a foot away from her. She propped her cheek on her elbow and grinned mischievously.

"Sooner than that," he retorted, cushioning the back of his head with his laced fingers. He closed his eyes, looking for all the world like a man prepared to take a long winter's nap.

"Don't go to sleep," Mary Kate fussed, getting wearily to her feet again. "We're going to have a picnic."

"A what?" He'd opened one eye.

"A p-i-c-n-i-c," she said, walking to the door and descending the three flights of stairs for what she hoped would be the last time for a while. She headed to the huge kitchen, now passably clean after Thursday's scrubbing down, and the refrigerator that wasn't quite old enough to be called anything so respectable as "antique." From inside it, she extracted the bottle of champagne she'd hidden there when Flynn was cursing his way up the stairs with the television set. She then scooped up the picnic basket sequestered in the pantry and ascended to the bedroom once again.

She stopped short in the doorway, surprised to find that Flynn had disappeared. Assuming that he was making use of the facilities down the hall, she set to work spreading a red-and-white checkered tablecloth on the section of wood flooring just in front of the fireplace, which unfortunately had no fire in it since she had yet to buy any wood. She planned on doing that first thing Monday morning and intended to pass the major portion of the time left until then in the bed under an electric blanket—once she'd finished unpacking and setting up housekeeping, that is.

Mary Kate turned in surprise at the sound of Flynn's footfall on the stairs and got to her feet to walk over to the door. Once there, she nearly collided with her partner, who was just stepping into the room, his arms laden with firewood. Grinning at her squeal of delight, he dumped it near the fireplace and then stood, brushing off his jacket, now dotted with snowflakes.

"It's really coming down out there," he told her, slipping out of the jacket. "Good thing I thought to get some wood delivered yesterday evening."

"What a sweetheart you are!" Mary Kate exclaimed without thought, already busy stacking wood in the brick fireplace.

Flynn grinned at her words. "Let me show you how to do that," he said, dropping to one knee beside her.

"How hard can it be?" she asked, nonetheless edging over slightly so he could reach the logs.

"Harder than it looks," he informed her, adding, "if you want a fire that's easy to light and will last awhile." He then demonstrated the ins and outs of placing the logs just so, and ended his lecture by using up half a box of matches before he got the fire to stay lit. Grimacing his disgust at himself, he murmured, "Thank goodness you won't have to rely on this for very long."

"What do you mean?"

"I'm going to buy the central heating this week. With a little luck the ductwork won't be as big a pain as I'm thinking it'll be, and we'll have some good, clean heat in time for your grand opening."

"You're getting central heat?" Mary Kate blurted. That was a major—and highly expensive—renovation she hadn't even considered when she'd made her mental list of things that had to be accomplished before she could open her shop. "That'll cost a fortune."

"It's only money," he responded, obviously surprised by her horror. "We've got a lot of winter left, and this place isn't exactly airtight. You'll freeze to death."

"No, I won't," she assured him. "I'll be too busy to get cold during the day, and I'll sleep under my new electric blanket at night."

"And what about your customers, once you open the shop?" Flynn questioned.

"I thought we could buy a wood stove for the shop. It would fit right in with the eighties decor I have in mind, and—"

"Wood stove?" Flynn exploded. "Are you crazy? Those are dangerous, Mary Kate, especially in a house like this. Why, you might as well be living in a tinderbox." He shook his head. "No wood stove."

"But—"

"And no buts." His smug expression told Mary Kate he expected her to concur without argument. And that rankled. Clearly, last night's easy victory had given him a false sense of security. Well, last night she'd been dead on her feet and upset to boot.

"I knew it'd be like this!" she exploded. "I just knew it."

"What are you talking about?" he demanded, rising to tower over her.

"That you'd be the only partner with a vote when it came to making major decisions."

"That's not true. I'm always willing to listen to your side of things."

"Sure, you are," she mumbled sarcastically, wondering just what other projects he had up his sleeve—projects he hadn't shared with her, projects that would double or maybe triple his monetary contribution to this partnership and reduce to almost nil her chances to buy out his share of the investment. She reached over to tug the tablecloth closer to the warmth of the fire and sat down next to it, Indian fashion, her bottom lip protruding in what could only be called a pout.

"I am," he earnestly assured her, sitting close by. "I really am."

"And always willing to *compromise*, too?" she persisted.

"Of course. That's what a partnership is, after all. A compromise."

"Good," she said with a quick nod. "Last night you got your way. Today I get mine."

He blanched. "But—"

"No buts and no central heating," she swiftly interjected. Then, determined to distract him from whatever rejoinder surely hovered on the tip of his tongue, Mary Kate snatched up her bottle of champagne, waving it under his nose. "Please, let's not argue, Flynn. I want to celebrate my first night in this marvelous house. Will you do the honors?"

Successfully diverted, Flynn took the bottle she handed him. Mary Kate dug out the stemmed glasses she'd packed so carefully that morning and held them out for Flynn to fill. That accomplished, they toasted to the success of their venture. Then, while Flynn watched in bemused silence, she drew out of her basket the bread, lunch meat, chips and pickles that would serve as their meal.

Flynn downed two sandwiches without any difficulty, all the while mentally replaying their last encounter. What the hell happened? he asked himself. Somehow Mary Kate had gotten her way again, and on a very big issue. He wanted to protest but didn't, fearing that she might go back on her promise to quit at O'Malley's just to spite him. He couldn't bear the thought of her in that bar with all those drunks ogling her. Besides, he would bring it up again later when he broached the subject of the antiquated plumbing, an issue he hadn't even raised yet, since it was all going to have to be replaced—and at a tremendous cost.

That rationalized, Flynn polished off a half dozen sugar cookies while Mary Kate gathered up the plates and folded the tablecloth. Though he would have loved to take a short snooze and even stretched out to do just that, the toe that tickled his ribs reminded him there was one major task yet to be done: setting up the bedstead. Mary Kate promised him she could handle everything else alone and that he could go home and catch his forty winks *after* he finished helping her. Grumbling good-naturedly, he got to his feet.

"Oh, please be careful," Mary Kate begged when he almost dropped the headboard a moment later. "This bed belonged to my great-great-grandmother. It's been passed down from daughter to daughter for five generations and even made it over from Ireland without mishap almost seventy years ago. I'd just die if anything happened to it."

"I'll be careful," he solemnly promised, his mind naturally wandering back in time. Mesmerized, he thought of the lovers who'd sought the haven of that bed through the ages, of the passions they'd shared, of the babies they'd made.

He glimpsed eternity and paled at his own insignificance.

"Are you okay?"

Mary Kate's question burst into Flynn's trance. He looked over to find her frowning at him.

"Fine," he murmured, self-consciously averting his gaze, trying to ignore the happily-ever-after visions spinning in his head.

Oblivious to his inner battle, Mary Kate worked on, humming softly. She reached for the linens, shaking them out and smoothing them—not such an easy task since the actual sleeping surface was a good foot higher off the floor than that of most modern beds. Still lost in his daze, Flynn stood motionless while she struggled. His eyes swept her slender form, lingering here and then there. He suddenly wanted to kiss her, touch her.

What would it be like to share this bed with her every night...for always? Flynn wondered. Thoroughly shaken by his wayward thoughts, he set himself to work, walking over to catch the corner of the sheet she had finally managed to spread, so he could tuck it under the mattress.

She smiled her thanks and ran her hand lovingly over the rose-patterned fabric. "I guess I'll pass this bed on to *my* daughter someday—" she laughed softly "—assuming I have one, of course."

Flynn could just imagine how a daughter of Mary Kate's might look—same sunny smile, riotous red hair, laughing green eyes. Again his insignificance hit hard. As attracted as she was to him, he really represented nothing more to her than the means to realize a dream. He would play no meaningful role in her life. He would never see that redheaded daughter. Something very like regret washed over Flynn, and a lump rose in his throat. Impatiently he swallowed it away.

Unaware of his inner torment, Mary Kate left him to spread the electric blanket while she went to go look for the quilted coverlet in one of the boxes still downstairs. Blessedly alone for the moment, Flynn stared down at the bed, his suspicious Irish brain half certain some kind of love spell had been woven around it—one that made unsuspecting bachelors crave hearth and home. Then, shaking his head to clear it of that foolishness, he reached for the blanket. Once it was in place he stuffed the pillows into their cases.

When Mary Kate still hadn't returned, Flynn sat down on the freshly made bed, bouncing slightly to test the firmness of the mattress. It felt so wonderful to his tired bones that he lay back and closed his eyes, lost in the nether world between days gone by and days to come; between now and never.

Mary Kate found him just that way moments later, stretched out and evidently sound asleep. Shaking her head at the sight, she crossed the room, determined to wake Flynn so she could send him home and finish getting settled in. Laying the comforter down, she walked around the foot of the bed to the other side. She stopped mere inches from where he lay, however, and stood without moving for several long moments.

How marvelously natural he looked in her bed, she decided, a disconcerting realization that brought vividly to mind her fantasy of the night before. Sensing Flynn would gladly make it reality, she sighed lustily.

"This is *my* bed," Mary Kate whispered, crossing her arms over her chest, "and I'm not letting you in it—no matter how tempted I am."

Flynn sprang to life at her softly uttered words, reaching out to tug her down full on top of him. Stunned, she didn't have the wits to struggle until he twisted his body, pinning her under his weight. Then it was too late. She couldn't move from where she lay, with her arms captured between them.

"So you're not going to let me in your bed, huh?" he murmured, brown eyes glowing.

"N-no," she stammered.

"Guess again," he whispered huskily, slowly lowering his head to brush his mouth over hers. His moist, firm lips demanded a response and she gave it to him without hesitation. Their tongues touched and tasted until she gasped for breath. Flynn shifted his position slightly, taking his weight on his elbows, a move that let air into Mary Kate's lungs and freed her arms. She wrapped those wanton arms around his waist and arched her body until they lay heart to heart, legs tangled.

It was Flynn's turn to respond, and he did, trailing hungry kisses downward over her cheek and chin and then to the racing pulse at the base of her throat. Mary Kate shivered at his touch.

"Cold?" he asked, raising his head to frown down at her.

"Hot."

Flynn moaned softly at that candid reply and rolled off her to lie back on the mattress, inches away from her. "There's a winter storm raging outside, Mary Kate."

"Yes, there is," she agreed, turning on her side to face him. She reached out, tracing his chiseled jawline with her fingertips, fingertips Flynn caught and kissed. He pulled her into his arms.

"The roads will be treacherous."

"Yes," she breathed, snuggling even closer.

"I could wreck my Jeep trying to drive home."

"Yes," she replied, placing a feather kiss on his chin.

"Why don't I just stay here with you tonight?"

"No," she said, but she sounded unconvincing, even to herself.

"You can't sleep alone—not in a bed like this."

"I can't?"

"You can't. It's made for two, Mary Kate. You don't need that electric blanket when I could keep you warm tonight." A fiery kiss on her lips proved the truth of that promise.

"And what about tomorrow?" she asked breathlessly, way past needing to be talked into anything.

She might as well have punched Flynn in the stomach. He stiffened in her arms and then jerked free, leaping to his feet to stride across the room to the fireplace, where he snatched up his jacket. Tossing it across his shoulder, he headed toward the door, halting abruptly just before he stepped through it.

Turning slowly, he met her bewildered gaze across the room. He gave her a sheepish smile and a shrug. "I just remembered we don't want each other's tomorrows, Mary Kate. I think maybe you forgot that for a minute, too."

With her heart sinking at the truth of his words, she nodded her agreement. "Good night, Flynn."

"Night, honey," he said.

Mary Kate didn't correct him.

Chapter Seven

By Sunday midnight, the third floor of the mansion at 9749
Pinkerton Lane looked downright livable, even to Mary
Kate's critical eye. The ornately carved bed, with its covers
now turned invitingly down, dominated the room that held
little else but her bentwood rocker, a bedside table draped
with a lace doily, and a six-drawer chest. The closet, added
long after the house was originally built, had been stuffed
to capacity not only with clothes and shoes, but with boxes
of memorabilia that Mary Kate intended to store in one or
the other rooms, once she got them cleaned and ready.

The gleaming mahogany mantel over the bedroom fireplace sported family photographs of every size, most of
them in antique frames she'd collected through the years.
Her plants were scattered all about, the majority of them
clustered near the bay window with its filmy priscilla curtains. All in all the room was a joy to behold, Mary Kate
decided, pirouetting to inspect her handiwork—a haven of
order and coziness compared to the rest of the house. And

though the wallpaper needed replacing and cracks webbed the high ceiling, she loved every aged inch of it.

Exhausted, she took a quick bath and donned her granny gown. She looked around for an outlet for her electric blanket, only to discover there wasn't one within fifteen feet. Unfortunately the cord on the blanket was only six feet long.

Snorting her disgust and vowing to buy an extension cord the first thing in the morning, Mary Kate fell into the bed, ready for a much-deserved rest. Since she'd doused the fire before retiring, the room, which had never been all that warm, cooled down rapidly. She tried to ignore the chilly temperature, but her cold nature wouldn't allow it. Squirming and shivering in the bed, she lay wide-eyed and wide-awake, listening to the night sounds of her new home. Every groan of the cooling floorboards and walls gave her new goose bumps. The howl of the winter wind trying to get in through the windows set her teeth on edge. The scurry of mice's feet in the crawl space overhead and the hoot of an owl in one of the tall trees outside brought vividly to mind vampires, ghosts and other specters naturally associated with stormy nights.

"Damn," she muttered, tossing back the covers. Obviously it was time for a cup of hot tea, a sure cure for insomnia. She reached for the bedside lamp, which she switched on. But nothing happened. Belatedly realizing Flynn probably hadn't been able to plug *that* in, either, when he set it there earlier that day, she fumbled for her chenille robe, which lay across the foot of the bed. Pulling it on more for its warmth than out of modesty, she slipped her feet into her fuzzy slippers and headed to the wall switch for the overhead light. Impatiently she flipped it upward. Again nothing happened.

Thoroughly spooked, Mary Kate glanced quickly toward the multi-paned double doors that opened out onto a balcony. She half expected to see the shadowy silhouette of

Count Dracula through the lacy sheers. There was nothing there, however, and swallowing hard, she stepped into the darkened hallway. A quick try of the light switch in that area produced no welcoming glow and told her that the winter winds must have downed a power line nearby.

Squaring her shoulders and ignoring the fear clutching her heart, Mary Kate made her way carefully down two flights of stairs to the kitchen and the flashlight she'd tucked into a drawer that morning. By the time she found the light and discovered the batteries were dead, she felt ready to pack her bags and head back to Boulder; or better yet, to Flynn's place, since he was a lot closer.

She wished for her soon-to-be-installed telephone and then thanked her lucky stars she didn't have it. Instinct told her that if she called Flynn, he would be at her door before she hung up and that sleep would be the last thing on his mind—or hers. Mary Kate remembered with chagrin just how badly she'd wanted him that afternoon—how badly she still wanted him. She remembered his taste and smell, the feel of his arms wrapped so tightly around her, and for the first time she actually began to understand how her mother might have been able to sacrifice everything for the man she loved.

Loved? No way. Mary Kate was far from that emotion in spite of the fact that Flynn had only to flash his dimpled grin to turn her brains to oatmeal. Yes, the man was irresistible. Yes, he could make her forget everything but the magic of the moment. But she was a big girl, for all that, and had no intention of abandoning her lifelong hopes and dreams to risk a fling with any male, especially one as dangerous as Flynn Rafferty.

Belatedly remembering that her cookstove was electric, Mary Kate reached into the dark interior of the refrigerator to grope for the half-empty bottle of champagne, hoping a small amount of it might relax her enough to sleep. Then with a juice glassful in hand, she headed back up to the bed that would surely be the warmest spot in the house. She sipped on the wine as she climbed the stairs and swallowed the last drop just before slipping between the sheets again.

But sleep still eluded her. Never had a house seemed so dark; never a bed so big, cold and . . . lonely. And it was all Flynn's fault. He had obviously found out about that weak gene of hers—the one that made her susceptible to Irishmen—and intended to take full advantage of it. Well, she would show him.

Mary Kate fully intended to hit the floor at the crack of dawn the next day, but her nocturnal wanderings, coupled with the overcast sky that hid the morning sun, had their effect and she didn't open her eyes until nearly noon. Groaning with disgust, she leaped from the bed and dashed toward the door and the bathroom where she'd left the baby-blue insulated underwear she would need to wear under her clothes to keep warm in the chilly house. Halfway there, she heard the clank of the door knocker downstairs.

Whirling back to retrieve her robe, Mary Kate hurried to the front door, arriving breathless and flustered. A quick peek around the curtains covering the narrow windows on either side of the door revealed Flynn, standing on her porch. Mary Kate finger-combed her mass of curls, wrapped her robe more securely about her and tied the sash in a double knot before she opened the door a scant inch.

"Morning," Flynn said, putting his eye to the crack so he could peer in at her. "My, my, don't we look bright-eyed and bushy-tailed today."

"Oh, shut up," she muttered.

He laughed. "I come bearing gifts."

"Oh yeah? What kind?"

"Food. I heard the power was out in this part of town, and knowing your stove is elec—"

He never got the chance to finish his sentence before a starving Mary Kate threw open the door and tugged him inside. "What'd you bring?" she demanded.

His gaze caressed her from head to toe and back again before he replied, "Chinese takeout." He gave her a rueful grin and shrugged. "How was I supposed to know this would be your breakfast?"

"Hey, Chinese is almost as good as cold pizza," she told him, snatching the white Styrofoam containers he held and leading the way to the kitchen. "And I didn't intend to oversleep today. I had trouble dozing off last night and then when I finally did, I overslept."

"So you didn't sleep, either, huh?"

She turned at his husky question, for the first time taking a good look at him. Though dressed for business as usual in a tailored suit, he appeared to be every bit as tired as she felt. "No. I had a little trouble getting used to the sounds of the house—strange place, you know—and my brain seemed to be stuck in overdrive."

He chuckled. "Mine, too. A penny for last night's thoughts...?"

She shook her head, unwilling to share them.

He took the food from her and set it on the counter. Then he caught her shoulders in one hand and placed the finger of the other under her chin, forcing her to meet his questioning gaze straight on. "Were you thinking about us?"

"What 'us'?" she questioned, twisting free to open a drawer and busy herself hunting silverware and napkins. "We'll have to sit on the steps to eat, I guess. I won't get a chance to look for a dinette set until later this week."

Flynn took the container she thrust at him and set it back on the counter along with the napkins and silverware. Again he reached for her, this time making sure she wouldn't get away so easily. "About last night, Mary Kate. I—"

"No apology needed," she magnanimously assured him. He *had* brought her lunch, after all.

His jaw dropped. "I wasn't going to apologize."

She couldn't believe her ears. "You weren't?"

"Heck, no. What do *I* have to be sorry for?"

"That little encounter on the bed, of course."

"Just how do you figure that?" he demanded, abruptly releasing her and stepping back, eyes narrowed in annoyance, cheeks stained a vivid crimson.

"Why if you hadn't *attacked* me, none of that would have happened."

"Hold on a minute!" he roared. "I never attacked you."

"Then what else would you call it?"

"I call it a near miss that would have been a bull's-eye if *I* hadn't done the noble thing and gone home."

"Are you saying I'd have let you—" she closed her eyes and took a deep breath "—let you..."

"Hell, Mary Kate, you were begging me to make love with you."

She gasped at his audacity. "You are surely the most egotistical man I've ever—"

"And you're the most fickle woman *I've* ever—"

"Fickle?" Mary Kate screeched her exasperation. "I am not fickle."

"Yes, you are—one minute warm and cuddly as a kitten, and the next, spitting like a wildcat."

Stuffing her hands into her robe pocket to keep from slugging him, she said, "I think you'd better leave."

"With pleasure," he announced, scooping up the food and whirling to head for the door.

"Are you taking *both* of those?" Mary Kate blurted in horror to his broad back, her empty stomach getting the better of her pride for one fatal second.

Flynn froze. Slowly he turned to face her, his incredulity written all over his face. "You're actually thinking about *food* at a time like this?"

Mary Kate cringed, suddenly realizing there might be a grain of merit in his accusation that she was fickle—well, not *that*, exactly. More like *befuddled*, and only when he was anywhere in sight. The rest of the time she functioned fairly logically. "Look, I'm sorry I yelled at you."

"And I'm sorry I yelled at *you*," he muttered, walking over to join her. With a half grin, he handed her a Styrofoam container. "Here. Enjoy," he said. Then he turned to back toward the door.

"Where are you going?" she asked, hurrying after him.

"You told me to leave," he replied with a shrug.

"I didn't mean it," she apologized and then sighed heavily. "And I don't really think you're egotistical."

"You don't?"

"No."

"Well, I don't think you're fickle, either. I'd say confused is more like it. And trust me when I say I know where you're coming from."

They stared at each other for a moment in silence and then both spoke at once.

"Flynn, I—"

"Mary Kate, I—"

"You first," she prompted.

"I didn't mean to, um, attack you last night," Flynn murmured, reaching out to brush back one of her errant curls. "I was only teasing."

"I realize that and I admit that it probably would have stopped there if I hadn't responded so—" she blushed "—well...you know."

"Hey, it was my fault. I take full responsibility," Flynn said.

"You can't," she argued. "It was my fault, too."

"But it wasn't. I—" He broke off suddenly, shaking his head. "Can you believe this? We can't even make up without fighting."

Mary Kate sagged in defeat. "How are we ever going to survive this partnership without killing one another?"

"Damned if I know," he replied, clearly as dejected as she.

"Maybe we should just call the whole thing off, go our separate ways, and—"

"No!" he exploded. He closed his eyes, visibly struggling with his emotions, and then opened them again. "No. I want to be your partner. We *can* do this. We can."

"Shall we give it one more try, then?"

"One more try," he agreed. His gaze dropped to her mouth, lingering there just long enough to melt her bones before he raised it again, clearing his throat. "Let's eat. I've got to get back to the office for a one-thirty appointment with the plumbers."

"Have you got plumbing problems at home?" Mary Kate asked, leading the way to the stairs.

Flynn winced and nearly stumbled over his own two feet. "You might say that," he murmured, squaring his shoulders and slowly trailing after her. "Mary Kate, we need to talk."

To his surprise, he won the plumbing battle easily. Mary Kate, who'd resigned herself with ill grace to rusty, luke-warm water, was only too willing to let him talk her into the modern pipes.

While they ate, she outlined her remodeling plans for the next two weeks, a schedule that included renting a steam machine to help remove the present, badly stained and peeling wallpaper so she could replace it, painting the door facings and trim, and patching the plaster on the ceilings. Flynn tried to talk her into letting him contract a professional to do the work, but she wouldn't hear of it, assuring him she had helped her parents remodel not one house, but two, and knew what she was doing. She then proceeded to prove it by describing, in detail, every step involved.

Flynn let Mary Kate's words wash over him, his eyes relishing the sight of her excited smile and sparkling emerald eyes. He thought of the night before and how close they'd come to making love. Though he'd congratulated himself time and again on his narrow escape, now, with his redheaded partner so tantalizing close, he found his good intentions on the line again.

Maybe if I kissed her one more time, he decided, his gaze on her full lips, I'd get her out of my system for good and we could keep this association a professional one. But no. He knew better. It would take more than one little kiss to purge his soul of Mary Kate. Why, a full-fledged affair might not even do it. Full-fledged affair? Hmm.

"Flynn?"

He started. "Did you say something?"

Mary Kate rolled her eyes in disgust and shook her egg roll at him. "Haven't you been listening to me? I asked if you knew where I might borrow a ladder."

"Why do you need a ladder?" he demanded, frowning.

"How else am I going to reach these ceilings? They're sky-high."

He glanced upward and winced. So they were, and she would probably break her neck or some other part of that gorgeous body trying to reach them. "I have a ladder, but you can only borrow it on one condition."

Obviously wary, she asked, "And what might that be?"

"You have to let me help you this week."

"But what about your business?" she protested, clearly as startled by his offer as he was.

"I'm off the rest of the week," he told her, omitting the reason why—a ski trip to Aspen he'd planned months ago.

He mentally canceled that much-anticipated trip, and without an ounce of regret. "I'll be glad to help. I *do* have a stake in this thing, after all."

"So you do," she responded, tilting her head to study his expression. Then she smiled. "Actually I wouldn't mind your help, if you'll let me be in charge of everything, of course."

"Of course," he smoothly agreed. "Now, I talked to a man this morning about the greenhouse you mentioned the other day and he has some prefabricated models he can put up, come spring thaw. I figured we could tear down that old garage and put it there, since the ground is already cleared, there's a water source, and it's pretty close to the house."

"Sounds good to me," Mary Kate replied.

"And I was thinking maybe you could hire a high-school student to help with deliveries. I have a client who has a really responsible son. He's done some work for me before."

"All right."

"Now, as for advertising—"

"That's my department," Mary Kate interjected. "And so is anything else that's left. I'm your *partner*, remember? Not your manager."

"Uh, right," Flynn admitted, feeling as if he'd just had his hand slapped. He kept his strong opinions about such issues as shop decor, bookkeeping, and purchase of the van to himself, sensing that another argument would surely result. He didn't have time to do even one of those justice right now; he had to be back at his office in fifteen minutes. He got to his feet. "I'd better hit the road. I've got a lot of last-minute details to take care of before I turn everything over to Tex."

"How are he and Jessie adjusting to married life?" Mary Kate asked, rising to join him at the front door. She'd been so busy lately, she hadn't had a spare moment to chat with her friend.

"Don't ask," Flynn responded wryly, grimacing his disgust at their moonstruck friends.

"What's wrong?"

"Nothing—in their opinion. Not only are they looking for a house, which they plan to 'fix up' themselves, they're already talking babies—" He broke off, suddenly remembering that he'd had that subject on the brain himself the night before and had just canceled a ski trip, of all things, and to help hang wallpaper!

"Oh, my gosh," Mary Kate murmured with obvious horror. "And Jessie was so set on getting her degree."

"According to Tex, she's still going to get it. He has visions of her going to classes with their little papoose strapped on her back."

Mary Kate cringed. "They've lost it. They've really lost it."

"Yeah, well..." He cleared his throat again, and avoiding her gaze, opened the door to step out on the porch. "I'll probably be back later with John Peterson, the plumber. You're, uh, going to get dressed pretty soon, aren't you?"

Mary Kate glanced down, suddenly remembering what she had on. She blushed. "Of course I am. I was on my way to do just that when you got here a while ago."

"Good," he murmured. "Peterson's got a heart condition and I wouldn't want to contribute to his demise." Then, before she could respond to the offhanded compliment, he winked, waved, and waded through the snow to his Jeep.

Mary Kate stood staring after him for as long as she could bear the cold and then stepped back, shutting the door securely. After cleaning up the remains of their meal, she headed upstairs to get dressed, impulsively sidetracking to the second floor, an area she seldom visited, since most of her big plans involved the first and third.

She walked through the spacious rooms—five, not counting the two baths—assessing possibilities. She tried to decide which of them would best serve as the master bedroom—if she were going to live on this floor, which, of course, she wasn't—and selected the largest. Encompassing the whole eastern wing, it would easily accommodate not only the bed but all the pieces that went with it, furniture now stashed in her parents' huge attic.

Lost in her daydreams, Mary Kate walked on, rediscovering the room next to that one, an area that would be perfect for a nursery. She pictured a baby, playing with his toes in the antique crib her mother had promised to give her someday. Not surprisingly, the infant was a boy and had curly dark hair and huge brown eyes.

She next visited what could easily be an office or study; a sunny, octagon-shaped room with built-in bookshelves on either side of the ever-present fireplace. The room next to that, she decided, would be perfect for guests, or perhaps as a playroom for that same precious baby when he started to toddle. Mary Kate crossed over to sit on the window seat, her eyes on the snowy yard outside, her thoughts on Jessie and Tex, their new home and their plans to start a family someday soon.

Envy stabbed at her; envy she couldn't deny since she recognized it for what it was, even if she didn't understand it. *What's wrong with me?* she mused. Her first priority before getting married and settling down was to succeed in her own right as a businesswoman.

But forever-after thoughts haunted her nonetheless. What if she didn't feel successful until she was forty? she wondered. What if it was too late to look for Mr. Right. What if she was too old to have that baby when she finally *did* tie the knot?

Then Mary Kate laughed softly at her own gloomy thoughts. Of course she would succeed. She had the dream, the drive and, thanks to Flynn, the wherewithal. Besides, she was young yet. Not only would she succeed; unlike her mother, she would have it all.

Meanwhile she would try to put all thoughts of romance right out of her head. It wouldn't be easy, of course, since Flynn would be by her side constantly for the next few days and he was undoubtedly the cause of her confusion.

Just how do I get him out of my system? she wondered. And then she giggled, remembering another obsession and how she'd unwittingly overcome it. When her oldest brother, Alan, now thirty-four, was a teenager, he'd purchased a heart-shaped box of Valentine candy for his girlfriend of the hour. Sternly forbidden to touch that gorgeous bright red box, Mary Kate, then a curious five-year-old, had slipped into his room more than once, fascinated by the lace and flowers that adorned it.

One afternoon, when everyone else was outside, her curiosity got the best of her and she opened it to find . . . chocolate—just her very favorite food in the whole world. Unable to resist tasting the "forbidden fruit," she'd stolen one of those wonderful candies and then cleverly rearranged the others so her theft wasn't readily visible. She'd then hidden behind the stairs and eaten every wonderful bite of it, certain her life of crime was over.

But it wasn't, of course. The chocolates haunted her, and the next afternoon she stole another piece . . . and another, until she could no longer disguise her evil deed. Panic-stricken, she ate all that remained, hoping her brother might think the drugstore had sold him an empty box.

But her brother wasn't fooled for a minute, of course. Not only did he yell at her, she had to reimburse him out of the allowance money she'd been saving for the state fair. And to top off her humiliation, she was deathly sick for two whole days. As a result of that experience, Mary Kate hated chocolate.

What if I overdosed on Flynn? she asked herself, her smile fading into a thoughtful frown. What if she had an affair with him? Would that get the man out of her system once and for all? Maybe, she decided, but what if her plans backfired and she fell in love? She could find herself married before she knew it. Such an experiment just wouldn't be worth the risk.

Or would it . . . ?

The next four days flew by for Mary Kate. On Tuesday, she and Flynn steamed off the old wallpaper, a messy chore that left them both tired and irritable. Wednesday and Thursday they hung the new, a softly flowered print that even Flynn couldn't fault. Friday, they painted door facings and trim.

By the weekend, the three-room shop had begun to take on a personality of its own. Caught up in the project, Flynn impulsively volunteered another week's assistance, which Mary Kate accepted since they were getting along so well.

They spent Saturday and Sunday apart by necessity, since they both had errands to run and personal business to attend to. By Monday morning, Mary Kate positively ached to see him again and actually hugged his neck when he got there, an impulsive move that surprised them both. She also offered to cook his breakfast every day—explaining that it was the least she could do, since he'd volunteered to help and then given her his all. He accepted the invitation, of course, and as a result, the next five days began with an intimate meal, shared over a table Flynn had brought her that first Monday afternoon when he returned with the plumber. After eating, they headed to the shop to put in hours of hard work before Flynn left in the evenings, each day a little later.

They talked as they worked, laughed as they talked, and actually formed a tentative friendship. Flynn, whose job it was to handle the technical end of things like business licenses, insurance and bank accounts, also advised her on what kind of displays and shelving she needed, her advertising campaign, and the grand opening she was planning. Ever mindful of their fragile peace, Mary Kate listened to his suggestions, graciously thanked him, and as woman have been doing for centuries, did exactly, and very discreetly, what she'd intended to do all along.

Meanwhile the plumbers plumbed and an electrician rewired the entire house, all this amid the clutter of boxes arriving daily—boxes filled with silk and dried flowers, decorative pots, ribbons, cards and baskets. Mary Kate greeted each delivery with joyous enthusiasm, and by the end of the second week the shop was a sight to behold.

Very nearly ready for business, its walls and display shelves were adorned with arrangements of every shape and size. The cooler, twice as large as the one Mary Kate had figured they could afford, stood in a corner, chilled and waiting for the fresh flowers that would begin to arrive early the next week in anticipation of the grand opening—now just days away. And in the opposite corner sat a shiny black wood-stove, a beautiful sight to Mary Kate, since it represented a major victory in their ongoing battle for control.

Late Friday afternoon Mary Kate waved goodbye to the plumbers, who'd finally finished their chore—the indoor part of it, at least—and plopped herself down on the stairs in total exhaustion, her head resting against the wall behind her. She didn't acknowledge Flynn's approach as he descended from the second floor where he'd just stored some plywood, until he collapsed beside her and stretched out his aching body.

"Was that John and his crew leaving?" he asked.

"Uh-huh," she murmured, shifting position and dropping her chin down on her chest so she could massage the muscles at the base of her skull. Flynn reached out, pushing aside her curls and taking over that delightful task himself. She purred in appreciation, a sound that shivered down his spine, activating every nerve ending in his body. "Oh, that feels wonderful."

Flynn didn't respond verbally, needing his whole concentration to keep his hands from dipping lower. Dressed in a curve-hugging thermal shirt and well-worn jeans, Mary Kate looked good enough to kidnap—right upstairs to that marvelous bed of hers. He'd thought about doing just that for days, but hesitated time and again, knowing full well that if she let him love her, it would be no one-night stand. He would be a goner for sure and find himself in Tex's mess: married, wanting kids....

But Mary Kate isn't interested in that kind of foolishness, he reminded himself, thinking of the many conversations they'd had that week. She'd shared her hopes and dreams and been adamant in not being ready for a long-term commitment. Did that mean she might be willing to indulge in a temporary liaison? he suddenly wondered. And if they *did* become romantically involved, wouldn't their mutual stubbornness and Irish temper ensure that they would be good and sick of each other by the time she was on her feet financially, and then part ways? Maybe, he decided. But was it worth the risk? Two seconds later, when Mary Kate reversed their positions and began a massage of her own, he knew it was.

"How about dinner tonight?" he asked, dipping his head forward so she could better reach his aching neck muscles.

"Are you kidding?" she asked. "I'm dead on my feet and so are you."

"So we'll go late, maybe nine or so. That'll give us—" he glanced at his watch "—four hours to clean up and recuperate."

"I don't know...."

"Come on, Mary Kate. We've worked our tails off this week. We deserve a break."

She leaned forward, resting her chin on his shoulder. "Where do you want to go?"

"Let me surprise you," he hedged, sitting on his hands to make them behave. "I *will* say that it's someplace special, so dress formal."

"Formal? Are you serious?"

"Dead serious."

"But I just have one dressy dress and it's, umm, not really appropriate for a restaurant."

"Please wear it," he told her. "The lighting will be dim, after all, and I want tonight to be special."

"Don't say I didn't warn you," Mary Kate said, thinking of her one and only gown, a daringly cut garment of shimmering emerald satin, bought to celebrate turning twenty-one. Delicately sprinkled with sequins from spaghetti straps to hem, the dress had attracted every man at her birthday party and outraged her overprotective brothers, just as she'd intended it to.

"It'll be fine," Flynn told her. He got to his feet then, groaning, and walked to the front door.

"Are you sure you're up to this?" Mary Kate teased.

"Trust me," he replied, with a mischievous wink that curled her toes. A second later he was gone.

Humming softly to herself, Mary Kate then made her way upstairs to that wonderful bathtub, which, when filled with the hot, clear water now available, would surely soak away her aches and pains, leaving her ready for whatever surprise Flynn had in store.

Chapter Eight

Mary Kate took pains dressing that night. Fresh from a two-hour nap that did wonders to revive her, she washed her hair and blew it dry in a vain effort to relax some of its natural curl. That strategy didn't work any better than it ever had, and grumbling her disgust, she caught her long tresses back into a vertical clip, instead. The result was astonishing, even to her own critical eye. Wispy tendrils framed her face and neck, setting off to perfection the tumble of curls cascading down her back and giving her a look of chic elegance.

Carefully applied makeup added to the illusion, and by the time Mary Kate donned her emerald earrings—a gift from her paternal grandmother—she felt positively regal. Grave second thoughts assailed her, however, when she stepped into the dress a few moments later and tried to tug it up over her breasts. She'd gained a good ten pounds since settling down from her hectic college days, and though she'd lost five of that in the frenzy of the past three weeks, five had remained, most of it topside.

Mary Kate found that "development" rather disconcerting, and a quick glance in the mirror confirmed she had every reason to feel that way. She looked like a woman hell-bent on seduction.

Is that what she was doing? Trying to seduce Flynn? Of course not! She had no such thing in mind. And besides, a man of the world like Flynn wouldn't even blink at the sight of such a dress.

She was right. Flynn didn't blink, but he *did* nearly swallow his tongue. His appreciative gaze swept her not once, not twice, but three times before he could speak. "*Holy* mackerel."

"I tried to warn you," she responded, blushing in spite of herself.

"So you did." He smiled that knock-your-socks-off smile of his and handed her a long, beribboned florist's box he'd had tucked out of sight behind his back.

Flowers? Stunned to her toes by the unexpected gesture, Mary Kate took the box and opened it, gasping her delight when she pulled back the tissue paper to reveal a bouquet of yellow roses. She curled her fingers around the long stems to lift them carefully from the box and then breathed in their heady fragrance. "They're beautiful. Thank you."

"I'd already bought them when I realized that you'd probably prefer something besides flowers from your date," he murmured. "I expect roses are old hat to you."

"Don't be silly," she scolded. "I love them and most people think just like you do. I *never* get flowers for any reason."

He laughed softly. "Well, I decided not to take any chances, so I brought this, too," he told her, revealing his next offering. "Chocolates."

"Flowers *and* candy?" The irony of Flynn's gift hit hard. Thoughts of obsessions, overdoses and the affair Mary Kate wanted but didn't want resurfaced, nearly overwhelming her. Highly flustered, she managed a wobbly smile, took the chocolates and fled to the haven of her nearby shop with a hasty explanation about finding a vase.

Once there, she laid both her gifts on the counter and stood gripping the edge of it in the dark, sucking oxygen into her lungs. *What's he up to?* she agonized. But she knew the answer before asking herself the question. Even a fool could see that Flynn Rafferty was "hell-bent" on a seduction of his own, and though not exactly experienced in such matters, Mary Kate was no fool.

She uncurled her trembling fingers from the counter and reached for one of the glass vases sitting nearby. With shaking hands, she put the roses into it, all the while reassuring herself that she couldn't be seduced if she didn't want to be. And *that*, she abruptly realized, was the problem. She wanted to be—badly.

"You *are* a fool, Mary Kathleen," she decided.

In a daze of confusion, she walked over to the sink to fill the vase, ever mindful of the splashing water and what it could do to her dress. That accomplished, she turned to rejoin Flynn, blossoms in hand. Two feet from the shop exit, however, she halted, knowing she had to *do* something, *decide* something before she stepped through that door to face her charming Irishman.

He wanted her; she knew it. She wanted him; he knew it. So, now what? she wondered. Resist? Counterattack? Accept?

"Mary Kate?" Flynn's concerned voice drifted into the shop.

"Just a sec," she called to him, stalling. What's the worst that could happen? she demanded of herself, though she well knew the answer: the forever-afters she'd dreamed about—only a little earlier than she'd planned. And what's the best? she next asked herself, quickly deciding that could only be a magical night in Flynn's arms.

She thought of his oft-voiced disgust for marriage or any long-term commitment and decided that was as good an insurance against forever-after as she could ask for. She then thought of the tickle of his mustache on her face, his hot kisses, his warm body; and squaring her shoulders, she stepped through the door, ready for whatever he might offer that night.

"There," she murmured, when the roses had been placed on the kitchen table. "All done."

"Then I guess we'd better make tracks," Flynn replied, glancing at his watch. "Our reservation is for nine and we've got just enough time to get there." He helped her into the fox jacket she drew from the hall closet and then turned toward the door, halting before he opened it to murmur, "You really look beautiful tonight."

"Thanks," she responded. She made an inspection of her own, noting with breathlessness his black tux with its satin lapels, which contrasted sharply with his crisp white shirt. The bow tie and cummerbund completed the picture of suave perfection and boosted her flagging courage. Any woman would be proud to be seen with him. She was one lucky gal. "You don't look half bad yourself, you know."

Flynn chuckled. "Thanks. I *did* try." He glanced at her strappy high-heeled sandals, clearly assessing their ability to keep her warm. "There's snow on the ground, Mary Kate. Your toes are going to freeze."

"Even if I had on mukluks, my toes would freeze," she reminded him, wiggling her partially exposed digits. "Besides, it's only for a few hours."

"And I'll help you warm them up when we get back," he promised casually. But his husky voice sent a shiver of excitement skittering down Mary Kate's spine. Her head flew

up. She saw the predatory gleam in his eye—one she knew
well; one that set her heart to dancing. And, certain she
knew exactly what she was doing, Mary Kate took his extended hand. Together they stepped out into the night.

They wined, dined, and danced...for hours. Mary Kate
felt like Cinderella, but when her "coach" finally carried
her home, it was well past midnight and she still had her
handsome prince, who showed no inclination to leave.

With her innocence concerning the opposite sex suddenly hitting hard, she stammered an invitation for coffee,
which Flynn smoothly accepted. Seconds later found him
sitting in one of her kitchen chairs, tie untied, jacket shed,
silent and watching every move she made. His bold gaze
shimmied over her like a caress. His glowing eyes told her
what he wanted from her.

Suddenly abandoning her task, Mary Kate kicked off her
shoes and went to him. Flynn caught her in his arms, pulling her down onto his lap, holding her tightly. She returned
the hug with abandon, relaxing against him, resting her face
on his shoulder.

"Tired?" he breathed against her neck.

"Wired," she corrected, tilting her head back so he could
find the ultrasensitive spot just below her earlobe.

Chuckling, he pressed his lips right there before nibbling
his way from one peachy shoulder to the other. "So...
am...I."

She could well believe that. The air crackled with ten-
sion; her flesh tingled to his touch. He raised his hands,
pushing aside the sequined straps of her gown, further ex-
posing the swell of her full breasts. His mouth trailed
downward, tasting, teasing, exploring. His hands were
magical, stirring her to shivery excitement.

Moaning softly, Mary Kate fumbled with the studs on his
shirt until she'd bared his chest to her eyes and lips. Her

fingers danced over his rib cage, tangling in the dark, curly hair liberally sprinkled there. Her tongue traced his collar bone, tantalizing him. He groaned in response. "I want to stay with you tonight."

"I want you to," she whispered.

Flynn pulled Mary Kate's straps back up on her shoulders, scooped her into his arms and got to his feet. He headed for the stairs, actually setting a foot on the bottom one before she came to her senses.

"You can't be thinking of carrying me up three flights of stairs!" she blurted in disbelief, wiggling to be put down. "My legs might be a little wobbly, but they still work."

"Honey, right now I could carry you to the top of Pike Peak," he cockily assured her.

"And what use would you be to me once we got there?" she demanded. "Breathless, weak and—"

Flynn burst into laughter and set her on her feet. "Actually, I'm that already, but you do have a point," he said warmly, visually assessing that her body worked just fine. Her heart turned over in response to the gleam in his eye. "I've wanted this ever since that first night at O'Malley's," he then murmured, claiming her lips in a kiss that left her trembling. When he raised his head again, his dark eyes smoldered with desire. He reached behind her head, releasing the hair clip. Her thick curls, freed from confinement, tumbled around her shoulders. Flynn heaved a sigh of satisfaction. "Don't count on getting any sleep tonight, Mary Kate O'Connor."

"Sleep is the last thing on my mind," she brazenly admitted, pressing her body to his. Suddenly sure that their lovemaking would be a rapture beyond her wildest imaginings, Mary Kate vowed that she would make the most of every passionate moment they stole. Whatever time they found for each other would be special—fiery and unforgettable.

Flynn stepped back and draped an arm across her shoulders, guiding her up the stairs. "We'll stay in bed all day tomorrow—God, what a luxury after this hectic week—and *maybe* get out just long enough to get my things."

"What things?" Mary Kate questioned in her naiveté, snuggling closer as they ascended the many steps to her bedroom.

"My clothes, my—"

"You're bringing clothes over here?" she interrupted, frowning slightly as a cloud of unease passed over her.

Misunderstanding the reason for her question, he chuckled and tightened his embrace. "Eventually I *will* need clothes." He looked down at her and grinned. "All right, you win. We'll get them Sunday. I'll see if I can borrow the truck again then, too."

"Truck?" Real alarm clutched her heart now. Surely he wasn't thinking of—? "Why do we need a truck?"

Flynn halted abruptly and turned her way, his eyes narrowed slightly. "To move my furniture, of course, not to mention my television, my stereo, my—" He broke off midsentence, his gaze searching her face. "What's wrong?"

"Nothing. I just, uh... Are you sure it's wise to move *everything*?" she asked with a calm that defied logic since a noose she just wasn't ready for had begun to tighten around her neck.

He frowned. "You don't want me to stay?"

"Tonight, yes," she told him. "But I'm not sure I'm ready to have you move in with me. I've got a lot on my mind these days with this grand opening just around the corner. I don't have time for a full-fledged relationship...."

"That's the beauty of it, honey," Flynn exclaimed, pulling her into his arms, gently rocking them both. He rested his chin on the top of her head. "I'll be here to help you every night. Heck, for that matter, I could do what I've been

thinking about doing for days and turn the rest of the firs
floor into offices. I'll move Advantage Finance Company
right into the house, too. Then I'll be here day *and* night."

"But Flynn—"

"I'll act as your mentor. Honey, your business problem
are over. With me to guide you, how can My Wild Irish Rose
be anything but a success?"

Mary Kate jerked free and glared at him. "Give me some
credit. I've worked hard the last few weeks, and—"

"Of course you have," he soothed, patting her shoulder
"And so have I. What I meant was—"

"What you meant was you never believed I had the brain
to run a profitable business in the first place, and you wan
to stay close by so you can keep an eye on me. Well, for you
information, I don't need your help." She took a step bacl
and put her hands on her hips. Her chest heaved in agita
tion, a motion that naturally drew Flynn's eye to her shad
owy cleavage.

"Look," he murmured, clearly having second thought
and now anxious to make peace. "Calm down. You'r
jumping to conclusions. Why don't we table this discussio
until tomorrow. I think by then you'll be a little more will
ing to see things my way, and besides, we've got better thing
to do tonight than fight." He reached out, brushing bacl
one of her errant curls, trailing his fingers over her shoul
der.

"Think again, buster," Mary Kate snapped, slapping hi
hand away. Every red hair on her head stood on end, read
to do battle. "I want you out of here—now."

He stiffened at her words. "What did you say?"

"You heard me."

"You're backing out?" he blurted in disbelief.

She nodded firmly and raised her chin in defiance
"You're damned right, I am. When I give myself, it will b
to a man who considers me an equal."

"I never figured you for a tease," Flynn muttered, his eyes suddenly hard as steel, his cheeks crimson.

Mary Kate gasped at the insult. "How can you say such a thing? I didn't tease you."

"Oh yeah? What about that little seduction in the kitchen?"

"Seduction? *Seduction?* You've got your nerve. Just who came in here tonight with flowers and candy? I'm surprised you didn't bring your clothes with you then. You were that sure of yourself."

He flinched.

"And for your information, I meant every word I said in the kitchen," Mary Kate continued, shaking a finger at him. "But never in my wildest dreams did it occur to me that you'd want to move in."

"Hell, Mary Kate!" he yelled. "You should know by now I never do anything halfway."

"And *you* should know I'd never agree to a full-time roommate," she retorted. "If I wanted a man around to 'guide' me, I'd move back to Phoenix or get married, for Pete's sake."

Clearly bewildered by this turn of events, Flynn didn't respond for a moment. Then his lips thinned with anger. He opened his mouth as though to speak, but clamped it tightly shut again, obviously seething. Fists clenched, he whirled on his heel, stalked down the steps and disappeared into the kitchen, erupting from that room in seconds, jacket and tie in hand, to stride to the front door.

He slammed the door when he left—a sound that assaulted Mary Kate's ears and reverberated harshly through the long hallways that were meant to echo with laughter and love.

"Tex? Are you awake?" Flynn pounded on his friend's door with his fist, ventilating his still-hot temper. "Tex!"

"I'm coming, I'm coming," a muffled male voice grumbled from within. Two minutes later, the door flew back, revealing Tex Charleston, dressed in a tattered pair of sweats, his hair tousled, his blue eyes clouded with sleep. "What the hell are you doing over here at—" the blonde looked at his watch and groaned loudly "—*two-thirty*?" His gaze swept over Flynn. "And in a tux, for God's sake?"

"I need to talk to you *now*," Flynn told him, brushing past to enter the living room. He stopped short a half step later, spotting Jessie, berobed and wide-eyed, standing in the bedroom doorway. "Evening, Jessie," he mumbled somewhat self-consciously. In his anger he'd forgotten her existence.

"It's morning," she calmly replied, unsmiling, "and I'm waiting to hear your answer to Tex's question."

Flynn ran trembling fingers through his hair and then gave them both a rather sheepish grin. "Uh, do you have any coffee made? I've got a doozy of a headache."

"Are you drunk?" Tex asked, walking closer to frown at his friend.

"Of course, I'm not drunk. You know I never drink and drive. Now, do you have any coffee?"

"Sure," Jessie responded dryly. "We always make a fresh pot in the wee hours of the morning. That way, it's good and strong by the time we get up."

Flynn winced at the sarcasm that successfully cooled what remained of his rage. "Hey, I'm sorry I got you two out of bed, but I've got a real problem, and Tex is the only one I know who can help me."

"Don't tell me. Let me guess," Tex said, walking over to the couch to collapse wearily on one end of it. "Your problem has red hair and the initials M. K. O., right?"

"Very funny," Flynn muttered, plopping into a nearby recliner. Tex looked Jessie's way and patted the empty cushion next to him, but the brunette shook her head, pointing to the kitchen before she headed through the door.

"So it's not Mary Kate?" Tex questioned.

"Oh, it's her, all right. That woman has got to be the most baffling, most stubborn, most infuriating human being on the planet. It's almost like she was born knowing how to get to me and spent her whole life perfecting the art until we met and she could practice it."

"What'd she do this time?"

"She ordered me out of *my* house, for starters."

"Yeah?" Tex's face broke into a grin of delight, which Flynn ignored with difficulty.

"Yeah, and that was *after* she, uh—" Flynn glanced toward the kitchen and Jessie, who was busy making coffee but well within earshot. He lowered his voice. "Indicated she wouldn't mind if I stayed all night with her."

"Let me get this straight," Tex boomed, clearly unperturbed by Jessie's presence. "Things were getting hot and heavy, she invited you upstairs, and *then* kicked you out?"

Flynn cringed at his bluntness. "Something like that."

"I take it she was angry when you left?"

"*Livid* would be more like it," Flynn answered, nodding his thanks when Jessie handed him a cup of instant coffee.

"So what did you say to make her that way?" the young woman asked as she settled herself next to her amused husband.

"Nothing, really," Flynn claimed. He took a long sip of his coffee. "We were talking about sleeping late tomorrow, or, uh, today, I guess. I mentioned getting my clothes moved and borrowing a truck for the rest of my things—"

Jessie gasped. "You're moving in with her?"

"That was the plan before she went off the deep end," Flynn replied, noting Tex's amusement had vanished and Jessie's chin had dropped. "What's wrong with that? People do it every day. I figured we'd set up housekeeping together and save some wear and tear on our cars, not to mention the convenience of having both our businesses right there."

"*Both* your businesses?" Tex asked.

"That's right. I've been thinking all week about moving Advantage over there. It would save me a bundle in rent and I'd be close by to help Mary Kate run her shop. You'd think she'd be grateful for the offer, but instead she went berserk."

"I can imagine," Jessie murmured, clearly horrified. Tex threw back his head, hooting with laughter, a sound that rasped on Flynn's already frazzled nerves.

"Will you shut up?" the Irishman demanded irritably.

"I knew this would happen," Tex said, choking back his mirth with difficulty. "Weeks ago, I told Jessie that Mary Kate would be the one." He glanced toward his wife and grinned. "Didn't I?"

"Be the one to what?" Flynn asked before Jessie could reply.

"Be the one to hook you," Tex told him. "You want to know why every little thing she says and does irritates the blue blazes out of you? You're in love."

"Go to hell."

Tex howled his mirth and got to his feet, gleefully striding across the room to his pal. He stood over him, chuckling, thumbs hooked in his elastic waistband, perusing Flynn's face with exaggerated interest. "Yep—" he nodded slowly "—you've got all the symptoms: bloodshot eyes, sweaty palms, that desperate look—"

Flynn leaped up to tower over Tex. "You're crazy!" he yelled.

"No. I'm *right*!" Tex yelled back.

They glared at each other, both breathing hard and ready to land a punch. Jessie sprang up, racing to referee. "Will you idiots just cool it! Some friend you are, Tex. Flynn comes over here for help and you *laugh* at him.''

Flynn smiled in satisfaction at the scolding, adding his two cents' worth. ''Yeah.''

''And *you*,'' Jessie continued, turning on him, ''have your nerve coming over here this time of night, whining because Mary Kate kicked you out of her house. Of course, she did. I'd have done the same thing.'' She crossed her arms over her chest and shook her head. ''Men! Who needs 'em?''

Both males gaped at her.

''Tex, I want to talk to Flynn—very seriously. If you don't think you can keep your mouth shut, I want you to beat it.'' Her tone indicated she would brook no argument, and Tex nodded to agree. ''Good. Now, both of you sit down, I have something to say.''

They complied.

Jessie began to pace the room, with pale blue robe billowing behind her at every step. Flynn risked a sidelong glance at Tex, who intercepted it and shrugged, but didn't open his mouth.

Then the brunette perched on the edge of the coffee table in front of both men. She looked Flynn dead in the eye and asked, ''How long have you known Mary Kate?''

''About a month,'' he told her, softly adding, ''but it seems like my whole life.''

''And you've been working closely with her for how long?''

''Two weeks.''

''Has she ever mentioned her dad?''

''Sure, she has,'' Flynn replied. ''He sounds like my kind of guy.''

Jessie winced. ''Has she mentioned her brothers?''

''Yeah, yeah,'' he muttered impatiently.

''Has Mary Kate talked about her mom?''

"Yes. No. I don't know." Flynn sighed. "What's your point, Jessie?"

"*My* point is that you've obviously had your head in the clouds so long you've missed *her* point. Why, I hadn't known that woman two days before I understood how she felt about macho men who think God put them on this earth to guide helpless females."

"*Macho men?*" Tex and Flynn blurted simultaneously.

"Macho men," she repeated firmly.

"I've never tried to 'guide' you," Tex asserted, clearly looking aghast.

"No, you haven't," Jessie agreed. "But you've given that poor little sister of yours a heck of a time." She turned to Flynn and shook a finger at him, adding, "And you've encouraged him."

Flynn and Tex exchanged a guilty look.

"Now, Mary Kate is a very bright young woman," Jessie went on. "She has a degree in business, years of experience in florists' shops, and an unbelievable green thumb. My guess is she found your offer to move in and keep an eye on her shop darned insulting. I know I would've."

A little insulted himself, Flynn cast his gaze on the patterned carpet, holding his tongue with difficulty, waiting for Jessie to end her lecture.

But apparently she had no intention of doing that just yet. "Mary Kate grew up in a predominantly male household. She knows her mother gave up her own career when she married, and has watched that woman slave for the men in her life. I believe Mary Kate has had it up to here—" Jessie slashed across her neck with a finger "—with the male ego. Believe me, a little of *that* goes a long way."

Jessie got to her feet and yawned. "Enough said, I think. I'm going back to bed. If you two jokers want to stay up the rest of the night and argue about whether or not Flynn's in love, that's your business. Frankly, there's not a doubt in my mind. I *know* he is." With a "So there!" nod, she turned on her heel and left the room, shutting the door securely behind her.

"Hell," Flynn muttered, glaring at that closed door. It was one thing to have his longtime buddy spout such nonsense; Tex did it all the time and usually to razz Flynn, who was now fairly used to it, if not always immune. It was something else altogether, however, to hear such a pronouncement from Jessie—cool, calm and collected Jessie—the woman who'd tamed one of the most dedicated bachelors since Casanova.

That "dedicated bachelor" chuckled and rested his head on the back of the couch. "God, I love her."

"Well, I don't love Mary Kate," Flynn told him, getting to his feet.

"Oh, yes, you do. You're just in the denial stage and not quite ready to admit it yet."

"I'm telling you, I don't!"

"All right, all right. Have it your way. You don't love Mary Kate, and I guess you decided to move in with her simply because you have a thing for hundred-year-old houses."

"No," Flynn snapped. "I decided to move in with her because I... I—" He broke off, suddenly unwilling to air the depth of his need for Mary Kate and his hopes that an affair would get her out of his system. He stuck his fingers into his jacket pockets and rocked back on his heels. "I decided to move in with her because I want her."

"Ahh," Tex said. "You *want* her." He stood and began to pace the room, hands locked behind his back. "Now we're getting somewhere. You...want...Mary Kate. That's simple enough, but where do you want her? In your bed every night?"

"That'll do, for starters," Flynn told him with a cocky grin.

Tex didn't grin back. "And I guess waking up with her curled up beside you sounds kind of nice, too, huh?"

Flynn shrugged. "Sure."

"I thought so," Tex said. "And you probably think sharing breakfast with her every morning would get any day off to a roaring start, and that dinner à deux would be the perfect ending."

"Maybe," Flynn murmured, his head suddenly filled with visions of Mary Kate, puttering around the kitchen in that sexy old robe of hers, hair in a tangle from the passion of the night before. He next pictured how it might be late at night, picnicking in front of the fireplace again, steps away from that enchanted bed or maybe even in it, lost in love.

Love? Flynn frowned.

"*And,*" Tex blithely continued, seemingly oblivious—or maybe not—to his old friend's mental turmoil. "You figure it would be pretty damn comforting to know she was somewhere close by if you needed her during the day. In fact, that's undoubtedly why you want to move Advantage."

Flynn didn't respond to that at all, now dead certain he didn't like the turn this rather one-sided conversation had taken. "That's one way to put it, I guess."

"It sure is. And there's another way, too." Tex halted his march inches from where Flynn stood. "You...love...Mary Kate," he said, punctuating every word with a poke of his forefinger into Flynn's chest.

"I do not, dammit!" Flynn exploded.

"Didn't you just admit you want more than sex from her?"

"Of course not!"

Tex snorted his exasperation. "Oh, yes, you did, and whether you like it or not, my friend, that's love."

Flynn swallowed hard. "It is?"

"You're damned right it is."

Tex's words rang like a death knell. Flynn stood in stunned silence, for the first time wondering if there might be a grain of truth—just a grain—in what Tex had said. Mary Kate certainly affected him as no woman ever had before, and he knew deep inside it would take more, much more than a few weeks or even months of her, before he would have had enough—if he ever would.

Tex apparently caught sight of his woebegone expression. "It's not the end of the world, Rafferty. Look at me. I'm happier now than I've ever been."

"You *do* seem satisfied," Flynn grudgingly agreed.

"Of course, I'm satisfied. I've got it all. And you can have it, too. All you have to do is marry that woman."

"Marry her! You must be loco."

"You have a better solution?"

"An affair. A nice, no-strings affair."

Tex hooted with laughter. "No strings? Hell, man, there's no such thing, and even if there were, you'd never be happy with that kind of halfway arrangement. You love being in control too much. Besides, how would you ever sleep at night, knowing there was nothing but mumbled promises to bind the two of you—that she might get sick of picking up your socks and be gone the next morning?"

Reluctantly, Flynn admitted the logic of that. He was a man who dealt in contracts; he needed the security of legal commitment. "But how can I tell her how I feel when I'm not sure myself?"

"You're still not sure?" Tex's accusing stare hit hard.

Flynn squirmed under the intensity of it and knew the time for truth had come. "I'm sure," he muttered with a sigh, surrendering his bachelorhood to Mary Kate for the second time, and this time *not* snatching it back. "Damn. What a screwup."

Tex chuckled.

"This isn't funny!" Flynn snapped. "If Mary Kate can't tolerate a no-strings affair, how on earth will she ever handle 'tying the knot'?"

Tex shrugged his unconcern. "I have every confidence that you can deal with her," he said, walking to his front door to open it. Chilly air permeated the room. "Now, I hate to rush you off, but Jessie's in bed, wide-awake and wearing that pretty blue—"

Flynn threw up a hand, halting Tex's vivid explanation. Absolutely the last thing he wanted to hear about was of beautiful young women waiting in beds. "I'm leaving. I'm leaving." He joined Tex at the door and gave him a sheepish smile. "Thanks for the help. Sorry I woke you."

"No sweat," Tex replied, glancing over his shoulder to his closed bedroom door. He grinned. "Actually, I think this is going to work out all right—for both of us. Now beat it, and try to stay between the ditches, okay?"

"Yeah, sure," the Irishman muttered, stepping outside. A second later Tex shut the door, leaving Flynn to weather the Colorado winter chill alone.

Chapter Nine

Flynn's Jeep may as well have been on autopilot on the way home. He covered the six miles to his condominium lost in thoughts of commitment, marriage and the redheaded daughter that might be his someday, if the luck of the Irish were really with him, and *if* he plotted his strategy. But where did he begin? he wondered as he entered his apartment and made tracks to the refrigerator for a cold beer. By telling her how much he loved her? By proposing the kind of partnership he'd *really* wanted since the first time he laid eyes on her?

Of course not, he decided, popping the top of the can. Mary Kate was going to need time—a long time—to get used to the idea of marriage. Meanwhile, he would have to live lonely and celibate—unless he could talk her into an affair, after all. That wouldn't be easy, of course. She'd made it very clear how she felt about them. Or had she? Flynn sipped his drink, replaying their last encounter on the steps. Actually, Mary Kate had admitted she wanted him for the night—far too temporary an arrangement for Flynn. Now that he thought about it with a cooler head, however, one night with Mary Kate certainly seemed better than none.

And if he played things cool, didn't press her, the one night might evolve into lost weekends together, the weekends into weeks, the weeks into months.... Thank goodness they were partners and he had all the time in the world for this evolution. He would just have to be patient—take his time—no matter what it cost him in lonely nights and misery.

Shaking his head in disgust for all those wasted hours, Flynn headed for the living room and his favorite recliner. Halfway there, the phone rang. He stared at the instrument for a moment before he set down his beer and answered it, knowing with certainty it wouldn't be Tex. That left only Mary Kate, undoubtedly as lonely as he was by now and calling to beg his forgiveness.

Flynn sighed his relief, certain that stage one was about to begin. He reached down to scoop up the receiver. "Hello?"

"Where have you been?" Mary Kate demanded, clearly agitated.

Flynn smiled outright, his usual bravado returning. "Why? Worried about me?"

She ignored that. "I've been thinking, and I've come to a decision."

He smiled even more broadly, certain he knew what that decision was. She wanted him back. He glanced at his watch, mentally calculating how long it would take him to drive over there, hop into her bed and begin the evolution of their relationship.

But that wasn't her decision after all. "I think it would be better for all concerned if we end this partnership as soon as possible. I'm going to buy you out."

Mentally coldcocked, Flynn bobbled the phone. "This is some kind of joke, right?"

"No joke," she solemnly assured him. "I intend to reimburse you for what you've spent so far and buy this house of yours, too."

"The house isn't for sale," Flynn said.

"But you've *got* to sell it to me," she pleaded. "I've done so much work on it, and it's perfect for My Wild Irish Rose."

"The house is not for sale," Flynn repeated firmly. "And just where do you think you could get that kind of money, anyway?"

"I have my resources," she hedged.

"The same resources you had a month ago when you came begging for a loan?"

"Look," Mary Kate snapped, "there's no reason to get nasty. Are you going to sell me your house or not?"

"'Not,'" he said, adding, "I like that old house and I intend to keep it. Besides, I thought we agreed that you would rent from me if we parted ways."

"That was if we parted amiably," Mary Kate told him.

"Just what do you call this?" Flynn demanded as casually as possible, determined not to reveal his sudden panic that Mary Kate would move out of his house and his life before he could plead for their happily-ever-after.

"You're not angry with me?" He heard her doubt.

"Naw," he smoothly lied. "I admit I lost my temper earlier, but I'm over it now, and believe it or not, I'd already decided it might be wise to split up. I was going to talk to you about it tomorrow."

"You were?" Clearly she hadn't expected to hear that. It seemed she figured he would rant, rave and come crawling. Well, it would be a cold day in hell before he stooped that low—forever-after or not.

"I was. I'll call my lawyer and try to get back to you on Monday."

"Thanks, Flynn," she whispered. "Oh, and there's one other thing."

Now what? Flynn wondered, reaching for the antacid tablets he kept stashed in a drawer in the oak end table. He popped two in his mouth, hoping they would untie the knots of anxiety that had just formed in his stomach.

"I want your solemn promise that you won't come around here until I come up with the money."

"But I'm your partner!" he exploded, nearly choking on the chalky mints.

"Only until I buy out your share of this investment," she replied. "Please do this for me. You know you won't be able to keep from offering advice, and we're liable to have another knock-down-drag-out fight. I can't tolerate another one of those. I need my full concentration. Now, do I have your promise?"

Flynn sat in stunned silence for a moment, realizing that "cold day" had come sooner than expected. He thought of how his life had been before Mary Kate—a maze of work and meaningless relationships. He thought of her sunny smile, her optimism, her stubbornness. He didn't know how he would live without her.

But he would—for now, at least. And soon she would figure out she wasn't going to be able to get that loan and would come crawling, ready to admit how much she missed and needed him—physically and fiscally.

"You have my promise I won't come by unless it's very important," he told her.

"That's good enough, I guess. I'll be waiting to hear from you, okay?"

"Sure."

"Good night, Flynn. Sleep tight."

Sleep *alone* is more like it, he thought gloomily, but aloud he just mumbled, "Night."

The next week was one of the busiest in Mary Kate's life. She worked hard, slept little and ate not at all. Her days were a labyrinth of last-minute details and advertising campaigns in preparation for her imminent grand opening; her nights an endless haze of loneliness and dreams of a dark-eyed Irishman who steadfastly ignored her. That hurt, even though she'd asked—no *begged*—him to do just that.

After a brief meeting on Tuesday morning following their ill-fated Friday night—an hour during which both of them remained clinically cool—Flynn had disappeared from her life. He didn't call. He didn't drop in. He might as well have fallen off the planet. Mary Kate couldn't believe it. Though one part of her was glad he stayed away, the other part missed him terribly. She wondered if he missed her, too, and came to realize that she'd secretly hoped he wouldn't keep his promise—would be his usual pesty self, would stop by and steal one of those toe-tingling kisses, would sweep her upstairs....

But no. That scenario was out of the question. Flynn wanted more than she could ever give; and the sooner she escaped from this partnership, the better for both of them. Thank goodness the figures he'd quoted on Tuesday were more than equitable and not nearly as high as she'd anticipated. Dissolving their business alliance could actually be a reality because Flynn had shouldered most of the remodeling expenses himself, claiming they were his responsibility as landlord. That gesture had touched Mary Kate and saddened her just a little, too, since it seemed to indicate that he wanted out of this partnership as quickly as she did—or thought she did.

In truth, Mary Kate became less and less sure of just *what* she wanted as the first lonely week sans Flynn stretched into an interminable weekend. And though she probably could have stolen a moment to go to the bank, she didn't, telling herself she was just too busy with next Saturday's grand opening, an event that had lost some of its glitter and had almost become a chore. Yes. Unbelievable as it was, Mary Kate's victory—her long-dreamed-of achievement—seemed decidedly hollow these days.

The following Monday, Flynn bought a local newspaper and found Mary Kate's first advertisement—an eye-catching announcement for her grand opening. He also heard a plug for the shop's unveiling on the radio on his way to work. He wondered all that week about her progress, imagining her up to her neck in the frenzy of last-minute details. He wished he were there to help, but coldly reminded himself that she didn't want him around.

By Saturday, the big day, he was miserably lonely and beside himself with curiosity. Though sorely tempted to drop in to get an eyeful, he remembered his promise to stay clear and contented himself with yet another drive past the old house on his way to work.

To his surprise, the parking lot already sported several cars. That pleased him. He didn't want Mary Kate to fall flat on her face—not, he told himself, while his name was linked with the effort. When he drove by again at lunchtime, it was full. A quick inspection on the way home that night revealed there were still cars at the shop.

Silently congratulating himself on his wisdom in setting up Mary Kate in this section of town, an area sorely in need of a good florist, Flynn went on home to celebrate her apparent success with pizza and a beer, eaten alone. He tried to watch an old movie on television, but found his concentration practically nil. He burned to know how Mary Kate had *really* made out on her first day. Had all those cars belonged to lookers or customers? Had the comments received been favorable or otherwise? More important, did she miss him as much as he missed her?

He spent a lousy weekend sulking around the house, and late Sunday vowed he *would* get a report on her success—one way or another. But how could he do that? he wondered. Mary Kate had asked him to stay away—to be a very silent partner.

Then an idea hit him. Personal issues aside, he knew Mary Kate would never turn away a paying customer. He hadn't sent his mother any flowers in a while and she loved them dearly. *Naturally* he would buy them from My Wild Irish Rose since he had a stake in its success—at least at this point. While in the shop, he would ask a few pertinent questions—a perfectly normal thing to do—and see for himself just how she was getting along without him.

Mary Kate couldn't believe her eyes when Flynn walked into her shop first thing Monday morning. He looked as wonderful as always, and she wanted to hug him, kiss him, and tell him how much she'd missed him. Instead she graced him with a casual smile and said, "Hello, there."

"Hello, Mary Kate," he replied, smiling just as casually. He perused the shop, now filled to capacity with fresh and silk flowers, real and permanent greenery, vases, pots, wall hangings and so much more—each item chosen with care and representing the fulfillment of Mary Kate's hopes and dreams. "You've done a great job. I'm impressed."

"Thanks," she acknowledged, oddly flustered by the compliment.

He glanced over to a corner of the room. "How's that awful old stove working out?"

"That 'awful old stove' is perfect," Mary Kate assured him. "It keeps the shop toasty warm."

"Do you leave the door of it open like that all the time?"

"No," she said. "Only when I'm freezing."

"That's all the time, then." He grimaced. "Just be careful with that thing, all right? And be sure to close the door at night, and the dampers, too."

"I will, I will," Mary Kate promised somewhat impatiently, though secretly pleased by his blatant concern. "I *do* realize the dangers of an open fire in a place like this."

"I hope so." Flynn shook his head, obviously still lost in his worry. Then he asked, "How's Brian doing? Did he show up like he was supposed to?"

"He did, and he's a joy," Mary Kate told him, smiling when she thought of the teenager Flynn had hired to help out. "He's a very responsible young man. And as it turned out, he's involved in the work-study program at the high school this year, so he's able to come in right after lunch. That really takes a load off me." An awkward silence followed her response, then she blurted. "Look, if you've come for your money, I'm afraid I haven't had time to fill out any loan applications yet."

"You haven't?" He sounded almost pleased.

"No. But I will. First thing tomorrow," she promised, adding, "And if my, uh, local resources don't pan out, I'll get in contact with Shannon. You remember my cousin, don't you?" Flynn nodded. "She's mentioned branching out several times. I'm sure she'll come through for me."

"I see. Well, there's really no hurry, I guess...." His voice trailed off into another awkward silence before he said, "Actually, I had two reasons for breaking my promise and dropping by today. I need to send flowers to someone."

"Oh." For some reason, that simple request flustered her even more. She retrieved an order blank from the plastic holder and grabbed an ink pen with fingers that shook. "What's your pleasure?"

"Uh, roses, I think," he answered, rubbing his chin, a chin she knew felt deliciously scratchy to the touch very late at night. He frowned. "Do red roses symbolize passion?

Well, it doesn't matter if they do or not. I want to send red ones. A dozen. No—thirteen. That extra one can be the promise of things to come.''

''But thirteen's an unlucky number,'' Mary Kate protested, trying to ignore her suddenly churning stomach.

He grinned smugly and tugged a corner of his mustache, the same mustache that had tickled her upper lip every time they'd kissed. ''Not for me.''

''I see.'' She cleared her throat. ''When and where do I send them?''

''This afternoon to this address, and put them in a really nice vase—none of that milk-glass stuff.'' He reached for a piece of scrap paper, borrowed her pen, and scribbled out a name and address.

Mary Kate kept her gaze on his face, steadfastly refusing to let herself snatch that information right out of his hand. Calmly she took the paper and glanced down at it just long enough to verify he'd written a woman's name, darn him. ''I'll do it up really nice,'' she said, nearly choking on her words. ''Do you want to enclose a card?''

''Yes.''

She handed him a gift card, on which he wrote a message. He held out his hand for the envelope and tucked the card into it when she gave it to him. Then he sealed it with a flick of his tongue, a tongue that could tease a bare shoulder mercilessly. Mary Kate swallowed hard and looked away.

''How much do I owe you?'' Flynn asked, reaching for his wallet.

''No charge,'' she said. ''You're still a partner, after all.''

He shook his head. ''How much?''

Knowing they were about to butt heads again, and not sure she could trust herself that close to him, Mary Kate told him. He paid for his purchase, accepted a receipt, and then walked around the shop for another fifteen minutes, examining every item on the shelves. Mary Kate's frozen smile had developed icicles by the time he gave her a cheery wave and left. She snatched the card he'd sealed so meticulously and retreated to the workroom, where she tore it open without one pang of guilt.

"Last night was wonderful. . . . Flynn."

"Damn!" she exploded, stunned to her toenails. She sank down on one of the high stools near the worktable, lost in gloom. No wonder Flynn showed no signs of distress after their weeks apart. *He* wasn't sitting at home, moping the way she was. No indeed. *He'd* hopped right out of her arms and into someone else's, darn him.

What did you expect? her conscience demanded. *You've never even told him how much you love him.*

Mary Kate gasped. "I do *not* love him!"

You don't?

"No. And I don't care if he wants to have a torrid affair with someone else."

Oh yeah?

"Yeah!"

"Ma'am, how much is this brass flowerpot?"

Mary Kate whirled on her stool, thoroughly flustered to find that she'd been overheard. She mustered what dignity she could, slid to her feet and walked to the waiting customer, determined to put Flynn Rafferty and his mystery love right out of her mind.

Meanwhile Flynn had problems of his own. Having just sent roses—thirteen rather expensive roses—to a fictitious woman, he now had to find Brian and extract a promise that the youth wouldn't attempt a delivery, thereby blowing Flynn's whole impulsive scheme to make Mary Kate jealous.

Flynn didn't really know why he'd stooped to such a childish tactic, since he'd walked into the shop fully intend-

ng to send an arrangement to his mother. He suspected it
had a lot to do with Mary Kate's obvious well-being. She
hadn't missed him a bit, from the look of things. And that
rankled, especially after all the nights he'd spent aching for
her, so he fully intended to show her how much she had
'lost.''

Right before the noon bell, Flynn drove to the high school
the boy attended. He waited by Brian's car, a mustard-
yellow Volkswagen that was easily spottable, and explained
his little "joke." Laughing good-naturedly, Brian agreed to
help out and even offered to deliver the flowers to the local
children's hospital instead.

That sounded good to Flynn. Pleased with his morning's
work and certain that Mary Kate would soon rue the day she
dumped the likes of *this* Irishman, Flynn returned to his
office. He worked that afternoon with a lighter heart, convinced his redheaded temptress would soon come crawling.
They would have their forever-after.

It was only a matter of time.

Later that day, a dejected Mary Kate watched Brian drive
off in her station wagon, loaded with the day's deliveries,
one of which was an exquisitely cut crystal vase filled with
thirteen of her most beautiful roses. Though sorely tempted
to stuff some dead carnations in along with them, she
hadn't, of course. She was too much of a pro to stoop to
such treachery.

Haunted by the possibility of Flynn making love with
another woman, Mary Kate was a borderline basket case by
closing time. She lay awake that night—tossing, turning,
and venting her frustration on her pillow. She told herself
she should be proud of sticking to the career plans she'd
made. No man had tied her down. She had her shop: she
had her independence. She was her own boss, doing what
she loved most.

And she was miserable.

She was also having serious second thoughts about her decision to buy Flynn out. Why? she wondered. *Am* I in love, after all? She asked herself that question time and again that week, but didn't answer it until just after Friday midnight. Cold and lonely in a bed built for two, Mary Kate finally faced the facts. She wanted Flynn Rafferty—badly. She knew he'd felt the same and had been, in fact, eager to move in with her, an easy solution to their mutual desire that now didn't sound nearly so appalling as it once had. So why didn't she just call him and say she'd changed her mind?

The answer was simple. She loved Flynn; he didn't love her back. And though an affair—short or long—would certainly alleviate her emotional and sexual frustrations, she dared not risk revealing how she felt about her Irishman. He would only use that knowledge to manipulate her until she no longer had any control over her destiny.

So, what now? Mary Kate asked herself glumly. But she knew the answer. As long as she was the only one in love, she would have to go it alone. That meant dissolving the partnership. And *that* meant she'd done the right thing—the only thing—after all.

The next morning found Mary Kate unenthusiastic about the day ahead and for more reasons than a week's worth of sleepless nights. She'd tried for three days to get a loan and failed miserably each time, since she simply didn't have enough collateral to be considered a good risk. Then, at the end of her fiscal rope, she'd finally reached Shannon on Friday night, only to be bombarded with her cousin's business woes—a leaky roof and a broken-down delivery van. Clearly there would be no monetary help from that quarter.

Brian called in sick around ten o'clock the next morning—not really a major tragedy since the shop was only open until noon on Saturdays now that the grand opening was out of the way. However, to add to her frustrations, she couldn't get the fire in the wood stove to stay lit for more than five minutes. Fortunately that wasn't a major tragedy, either, since she'd dressed for the weather and not one customer had darkened her door thus far that day.

But what else could possibly go wrong? she mused gloomily, watching the snow falling outside her window. As though in reply to her question, Flynn stepped into the shop, dressed in that aged leather jacket of his and looking for all the world like a WWI pilot ready to swoop down from the skies to snatch her heart.

He greeted her with a cocky smile that grew even broader when his dark eyes swept over her, noting, she was certain, the purple shadows of worry under her eyes that no amount of makeup could conceal. Mary Kate straightened from where she'd been standing, elbows propped, behind the checkout counter. She squared her shoulders and mustered her brightest smile, determined not to reveal the anguish she'd endured at this man's expense, or the easy accessibility of said heart—should he really be interested in such a snatch.

"Good morning," Flynn said when he reached Mary Kate.

"Why, good morning," she brightly replied. "How in the world are you?"

"Wonderful," he said. "How's business?"

"Booming," she told him. "I haven't had a spare second to myself all week. I was so busy, in fact, that I never even had a chance to get to the bank about a loan." She gave him a teasing smile. "I don't suppose you'd be interested in selling out on the installment plan? It'd only take a hundred years or so and—"

"Sounds good to me," Flynn interjected.

Mary Kate's jaw dropped. "Are you serious?" she blurted, floored by his agreement to a suggestion made in

jest. Was he having second thoughts about their parting o
maybe even beginning to miss her as much as she misse
him? Had she misinterpreted the roses? Were they merely
thank-you for a romantic dinner and not a night of pas
sion? Her spirits soared at the mere idea.

"Sure. I'm not pressed for the money." Flynn drumme
his fingers on the countertop and glanced toward the cooler
"And speaking of money, I'd like to buy another bouque
for my, um, friend. Something different, this time. Do yo
have a suggestion?"

Twice in one week? So much for the romantic-dinne
theory. No man gave a woman that many roses because sh
had a healthy appetite. Spirits now sky-diving, Mary Kat
pivoted abruptly to walk to the cooler. She yanked open th
door and peered inside. "How about an arrangement o
daisies or carnations?"

Flynn frowned. "Naw, not classy enough."

"A plant, maybe?"

He shook his head. "No. I guess I'll stick to the rose
after all. How about yellow ones this time?"

Yellow...just like the roses he'd given *her*. Seething at th
injustice of it all, Mary Kate returned to the counter to fi
out the order blank. Just as before, Flynn wrote a messag
on the card she automatically passed to him and then tucke
it into an envelope. He sealed it, paid her and turned t
leave.

"So how are things with you these days?" Mary Kat
blurted to his back, unwilling to let him disappear so soor
She snatched a rubber band out of the plastic container o
the counter and twirled it around her fingers in an attemp
at nonchalance.

Flynn turned and shrugged. "Busy," he said, adding
"but no new partnerships."

"Oh?"

He grinned. "At least not the business kind."

"Oh." Resisting the urge to aim the rubber band for a spot right between those chocolate-bar eyes of his, Mary Kate set it aside and busied herself straightening the already immaculate desk. "Well, it was nice talking to you. I'll see that these are delivered today."

He took the hint. "Thanks. Tell Brian hello."

"Sure."

This time Mary Kate didn't open the card or read it when he left, certain that another "last night" sentiment would surely be the death of her—or Flynn, if she got her hands on him. Lost in a gloom that could only be the result of a broken heart, she walked back to the workroom to fill his order.

In her mind she replayed the moments they'd spent together, most of them tempestuous. How she missed their battles of wills and those noisy fights! What she wouldn't give for another stormy encounter that might end with a fiery kiss to patch things up. Did Flynn miss those things, too? she wondered. Was his new love the soft-spoken type? A "yes" woman he could mold and dominate?

There's one way to find out, she abruptly decided, actually thankful Brian had called in sick. She would make Flynn's delivery herself, and she would find out exactly what kind of woman she'd lost him to.

Two and a half hours, a city map and a stop at the nearest gasoline station later, Mary Kate gave up her mission. She sat in her car, motor running, staring at the name and address she'd copied from her records and wondering how in the heck Brian had ever made his delivery the week before. According to the very nice mechanic inside the garage, no such street existed. A quick check of the phone book had revealed that no such woman did, either.

On the off chance that she'd left a stone unturned, Mary Kate backed her station wagon onto the street and headed for the now-closed flower shop to recheck her information. Just as she arrived, the mailman did, too. Smiling a greeting and her thanks, Mary Kate tucked her purse under an arm, and took the stack of mail he handed her.

Juggling her load, she inserted her key into the lock and stepped indoors, only to catch the toe of her boot on the metal weather-stripping underfoot. Envelopes of every size and color flew into the air, as did her leather clutch bag.

Cursing her clumsiness and everything else in general, Mary Kate slammed the door and walked over to the stairs, sinking down on the bottom step. She struggled with tears for several long minutes before she found the energy to get down on her hands and knees, collecting the contents of the purse she never, ever fastened and the mail that was probably just more bills, bills, bills.

But one of her letters looked like an invitation. Curious, Mary Kate walked back to the stairs to sit. She slipped her finger under the flap of the heavy, buff-colored envelope to break the seal. Then she pulled out a card, elegantly embossed with the logo of the local children's hospital, and not an invitation at all.

"Dear Ms. O'Connor," read the neatly penned message in what was undoubtedly feminine handwriting. "Thank you so much for your gift of roses on Monday."

Roses? Mary Kate frowned, absolutely certain she hadn't sent out any roses on Monday except Flynn's. Puzzled, she read on. "Your generosity warmed the hearts of our patients and visitors alike."

There must be some kind of mistake, she decided. Reaching for the envelope, she double-checked the address on it—her own. Really confused now, Mary Kate turned her eyes to the note again. "Since I collect crystal, I was particularly struck by the quality of the vase. I plan to stop by your shop very soon to see what other items you might have in this line. Good luck with your new endeavor." It was signed by the director of the hospital.

Crystal vase? That cinched it. Those were Flynn's roses, all right, undoubtedly delivered to some hospital instead of to his lady love. What a disaster! Brian must have mixed up the orders—

"Wait a minute," she said aloud, sitting bolt upright, her brows knitted in thought. Brian hadn't even *had* any flowers to deliver to the hospital, so there couldn't have been an accidental switch in bouquets. Besides, Flynn surely knew by now that the roses hadn't been received. Why hadn't he complained?

Mary Kate pressed her fingertips to her temples, trying to relieve the throbbing pain there. Her mind aswirl with half-formed theories, she closed her eyes to better concentrate, to follow one idea through to a logical conclusion. But there *was* no logical conclusion, and thoroughly bewildered, she decided to call Brian for an explanation. Five minutes later she slammed the receiver down and shrieked her rage.

"How could Flynn do such a thing!?" she exploded, pacing the wooden floor in her agitation. "And to think I was actually jealous. Damn his lying hide!"

She thought of the nights she'd lain in her bed aching for his touch, of the doubts she'd wrestled with as a result— doubts about her career and her future. Obviously Flynn had figured out how she felt about him and was doing just as she'd known he would do—using that knowledge to manipulate her.

"Well, I've got news for him," she vowed with a vengeful nod. "I will not be manipulated and he's going to rue the day he tried to match wits with the likes of *this* colleen!"

Chapter Ten

Today's the day, Flynn told himself as he stepped into My Wild Irish Rose seconds before closing time on Monday. *One more bogus delivery, and she's mine.*

He paused just inside the shop, letting his snow-blinded eyes adjust to the dimmer light indoors. When the pungent smell of burning wood immediately assailed him, he glanced toward the stove. He noted that Mary Kate had, as usual, crammed it full of split logs, one of which protruded, and left the door of that blazing furnace standing wide open, no doubt in an attempt to get warm. He wondered briefly why she didn't just put on more clothes, but one glance in her direction told him she'd done the best she could.

Dressed in a bulky ski sweater, thick corduroy pants and knee-high boots, Mary Kate looked ready for a hike up the Alps. Wishing he dared suggest a less adventuresome way to warm her, Flynn approached the counter where she stood, ringing up a sale. Intent on her business, she hadn't spotted him yet, so he made use of the extra seconds to look around the room. He noted that there were two people in the shop and that they both seemed to be buying. Clearly things were going well here—and without his help. That only made his mission more difficult.

Flynn shifted his gaze back to Mary Kate. He saw that the bloom had disappeared from her cheeks, and he smiled to himself in satisfaction. She looked tired—as if she might have spent a few sleepless nights of her own. That idea lifted his spirits again and told him that his feeble attempt to make her jealous was working. When he got through with her to-day, she would be eager to admit how much she missed, wanted and, if he were really lucky, loved him. Tonight would surely find them together in that marvelous bed of hers, both warm as toast and well on their way to whatever kind of "forever-after" he could wangle out of her.

Vastly encouraged by that tempting scenario, Flynn walked to the counter. Mary Kate, just finishing with her two customers, looked his way and smiled a warm greeting. "Hi. I'll be with you in a minute."

"No hurry," he said, relishing the unmistakable welcome in her voice. So far so good. He glanced at his watch, suddenly inspired. "It's after six. Want me to lock up for you?"

She looked at the clock on the wall, shook her head in obvious disbelief, and said, "Would you mind? I had no idea it was so late."

Whistling cheerily, Flynn followed the exiting customers over to the door so he could secure it. Once they were outside, he changed the Open sign to read Closed, flipped the lock, and rejoined Mary Kate at the counter, pleased he'd so cleverly ensured a little privacy for them.

"How's it going?" she asked, glancing up from the order pad on which she still wrote.

"Just great," he responded. He flashed his most devastating smile, the one he saved for special occasions, and

leaned an elbow on the counter between them. "How wa
your weekend?"

"It was *fantastic*," she gushed, putting down her penci
and stretching lazily.

"Yeah?" That wasn't exactly the reply he'd expected.

"Oh, yeah. And yours?"

"Uh, special," he said, recovering with difficulty. "Reall
special. So special, in fact, that I'd like to send mor
flowers."

"Oh. Lucky lady," crooned Mary Kate, smiling serenel
at him. She flipped to a new page in the order book an
picked up her pencil. "Roses again?"

Disconcerted by her enthusiasm, Flynn hesitated befor
murmuring, "Sure. Why not? Got any pink ones?"

"I'll check."

Flynn watched as she walked over to the cooler to pee
inside it, wondering at her good mood. Saturday, he woul
have sworn his fictional love life was getting her down
What on earth could have happened over the weekend t
change things? Had she met someone, a male some
one...? His stomach twisted at the thought.

"Sorry, only five pink ones," she said, rejoining him. "
do have a dozen red or yellow, and six white." She shrugged
"I didn't expect to send so many out this week. Obviousl
if you're going to keep this up, I'll have to double my ros
order." She laughed at her little joke.

Flynn wasn't in the least amused, however, feeling dea
certain she *had* met a man—one who knew what to say t
make her feel appreciated. Silently cursing his own inabi
ity to do that, he murmured, "Go ahead and send red again
then. They went over well the last time."

"I'm *awfully* glad to hear that. I put them in my be:
crystal vase, you know, just like you asked me to."

She thrust an enclosure card at Flynn without taking he
eyes off the order blank on which she wrote. More than

little miffed by her nonchalance, he couldn't even think of anything to pen.

"Same address, of course," she said, busily writing.

"Same address."

"Good. I'll deliver them myself first thing tomorrow."

Flynn started. "What did you say?"

"I said I'd deliver them tomorrow," she murmured, glancing up. "I don't make deliveries after four in the afternoon unless it's an emergency," she added by way of explanation.

"*You're* making the deliveries now?" Flynn somehow found the wits to ask.

She nodded absently. "Only temporarily. Brian's still sick."

Flynn's heart leaped into his throat. "*Still* sick?"

"Uh-huh. He has a nasty cold, poor thing. Luckily I wasn't very busy Saturday and managed all right without him."

"*You* made the deliveries Saturday?"

"That's what I just said."

"And my roses were one of them?"

"Of course."

"To the address I gave you last Monday?"

"Yes." She opened her mouth as though to question his sudden interrogation, but he didn't give her a chance.

"How did you ever manage to find your way around own?"

"I have a city map. Didn't have a bit of trouble. Is something wrong?"

Flynn stared at her without speaking, his mind in overdrive. The name and address he had given Mary Kate were fictitious—or so he'd thought. But what if they weren't...? What if he'd accidentally made up real ones and some strange woman had gotten roses with his name on the card...?

He cringed at the thought. "Would you verify that name and address, please?"

"Why?" Mary Kate blurted. "You wrote it yourself."

"Just give it to me!"

"Okay, okay," she mumbled, hastily reaching into her order box. She extracted a card and read the name and address of the mayor's wife.

"*What?*"

She read it again.

"Holy—!" Flynn snatched the card to verify that Mary Kate had, indeed, sent roses to the city's first lady—roses with his name and some idiocy about wonderful last nights scrawled on it. But there was no name on the card and no address.

Eyes narrowed, he read the neatly penned message from the director of the children's hospital. He remembered Brian's offer to deliver Monday's roses to that hospital, and gradually the meaning of the note sank in. He raised his gaze, intercepting Mary Kate's accusing glare.

"Well?" she demanded hotly. "What do you have to say for yourself?"

"I, uh . . ." What could he say? That he was crazy in love and hadn't been acting rationally since the moment he first laid eyes on her? Not that. Not now. He swallowed hard. "I see you've discovered my little joke."

"*Joke?* What kind of idiot do you think I am? You did that to make me jealous, and you know it!"

"All right. I admit it," Flynn said. "I *was* trying to make you jealous. Did it work?" he asked with a lopsided grin.

"Don't flatter yourself!" Mary Kate exploded. Then she clutched the edge of the table, visibly struggling for control of her volatile temper. Long seconds and several deep breaths later, she said, "I can't believe you'd do such a thing. It was childish, manipulative and unforgivable."

He winced. "Don't say that. You have to forgive me."

"Give me one reason—one *good* reason—why," she told him, eyes flashing.

"Because I love you."

"That's not good enough—" she retorted, then she stiffened with shock. "What did you say?"

"I love you. And I didn't mean to hurt you. I'd never do that. I just thought if I could make you jealous you might realize what we could have together and—" he hesitated, suddenly terribly insecure "—love me back."

Mary Kate made a strangling sound and sat with a plop on the stool behind her. She brushed visibly quaking fingers through her curls. "Do you have any idea what I've been through this past week?"

"Hell?" he prompted hopefully.

"*Pure* hell." She shook her head. "I should run you right out of here."

"But you won't."

"No, I won't," Mary Kate told him with a disgusted sigh. "I'm too relieved you aren't seeing another woman. And I love you too much to risk never seeing you again."

Flynn caught his breath. He didn't deserve such luck. Tugging Mary Kate to her feet and into his eager arms, he pressed his lips to hers with a hunger born of wasted days and long, lonely nights. She responded with the same urgency, molding herself to him, returning his fiery kiss in full measure.

Flynn gloried in the sweetness of her, and teased her lips apart with his tongue, deepening the contact. Mary Kate moaned softly in response, a sound that stole what was left of his control. Flynn trailed his lips over her cheek to her earlobe, rewarded for his explorations by another low moan and a sexy little shiver that set his soul afire. "Let's go upstairs right now and make up," he whispered urgently into her ear.

Mary Kate laughed and framed his face with her hands. "You're incorrigible, Flynn Rafferty."

"Yeah, and you love me for it," he bragged with courage born of an emotional high. He took her elbow, propelling her none too gently to the stairway that led to the closest thing to paradise he knew. Just before they ascended, he turned, blocking her path. "You're not going to back out again, are you? I don't think I'm up to another cold shower."

"Maybe I should," Mary Kate countered saucily. "Heaven knows, you deserve a little misery." She pursed her lips, frowning thoughtfully.

Swiftly Flynn captured those tantalizing lips in a sound kiss.

"On second thought," Mary Kate murmured when he raised his head, long moments later, "maybe I shouldn't, especially now that I've finally gotten used to the idea of having you underfoot day and night."

Flynn grinned his pleasure at her admission. Clearly he was making progress—so much, in fact, that he found himself impatient to tell her what was *really* on his mind. The last few minutes with Mary Kate had convinced him that he would never be able to settle for any arrangement as temporary as an affair, even if it was a critical evolutionary step to the marriage he desired. "Mary Kate, I have some questions to ask you. They're important."

"All right."

He sat on one of the lower steps and pulled her down into his lap, holding her tightly against his thudding heart. "Do you forgive me for acting like such a jerk this past week?"

"I must be crazy, but I do," she replied.

His thoughts on what he still had to say, Flynn barely acknowledged her lighthearted words. "And are you going to let me move in with you?"

"Not before tomorrow," she told him, easing free to get back to her feet. "I've got other plans for tonight—speaking of which, we're wasting valuable time here."

Flynn didn't respond to her teasing. Instead he caught her hand, tugging her back down. "Just one more question." He cleared his throat nervously, sent up a prayer and plunged ahead. "Will you marry me?"

Mary Kate tensed in his arms and turned so she could read his expression.

"Yes, I really said 'marry,'" he told her in reply to her unasked question.

Eyes wide, she sprang out of his embrace, putting several feet between them. "Are you insane?"

Flynn rose to join her. "No, I'm in love. I know you think this is coming out of the blue, but I've really been doing a lot of soul searching the past few days. I've come to realize I'll never be happy with a halfway relationship. I want it all, honey: the house, the babies, the in-laws—"

"I can't believe you're saying this to me," Mary Kate exploded, clearly horrified. "You know I want to establish my career before I take on that kind of responsibility."

"But you just told me I could move in with you," he argued. "What's the difference?"

"A little piece of paper called a marriage certificate, that's what," she replied. "They don't come with escape clauses, and you surely remember how I feel about those."

"In other words, you want an easy out if I cramp your style."

"That's not fair and you know it! The time just isn't right for me now."

"And what am I supposed to do while you're becoming businesswoman of the year? I'm thirty-three. Most men my age are already married, with a kid or two."

"And most women my age are still in college," she retorted hotly.

That truth hit home—hard. "Okay, okay," Flynn murmured, holding his hands up to calm her. "We're getting off track here. All I did was propose marriage. I never asked you to give up your career."

"I know you didn't, and maybe you'd be satisfied with a part-time wife. But what if I got pregnant? Would you still feel the same?"

"I, uh, sure," he stammered.

"Well, maybe *you* would, but I wouldn't," she told him, "I have strong feelings about motherhood. That's not a role I could ever take lightly." She sighed. "Oh, Flynn, can't you see how it is with us? You're always one step ahead of me, asking for more than I can give, and then manipulating me into giving it anyway."

"I don't do that," he argued.

"Yes, you *do*," she countered. "Just think of the pains you took to make me jealous."

He flushed under her censure. "I didn't mean any harm."

"I know you didn't," she told him. "But the facts are still the same. When you don't get your way, you start to press. And since I'm not that strong where you're concerned, I give in. Nothing would change if we got married."

Flynn registered her words with a sinking heart. Taking into consideration some of his antics since meeting her, he realized she had every reason to believe as she did. And if the truth were really known, he couldn't be sure she wasn't right in her assessment of the situation. Sensing defeat, he considered the option she offered him—the affair he'd wanted so badly himself, at one time. Could he settle for that now? he wondered, watching her swipe at a tear snaking down her face. Could he survive, knowing she might walk out of his life at any moment, taking his heart with her?

He knew he couldn't. Tex had been right when he said Flynn needed the security of legal ties. So, what now? he asked himself. Give up? Go home to face another interminable night alone? Pain tore through him at the thought. "No marriage is easy. There's always give-and-take."

"We're both takers."

"Honey, I don't know any woman who gives more. And I can change."

"But you won't. And despite what you say, neither will I. I need time to think about all this, Flynn. I need to be alone."

Flynn closed his suddenly misty eyes and drew a shaky breath. Short of begging, there was nothing else he could do or say at this moment, and Flynn Rafferty never begged. Nodding briefly, he walked to the door. There he hesitated, already aching with loneliness.

"Good night, Flynn," Mary Kate said, gently urging him on.

He squared his shoulders and reached for the doorknob. "Goodbye," he answered without turning around. Then he stepped out the door.

Mary Kate couldn't bear to return to the shop that night. She stuck her hand just inside the door, groping on the wall for the light switch that would plunge the embodiment of her dreams into darkness.

Eyes blurred by tears, she stumbled to the kitchen from habit, and then turned on her heel to leave it again when she realized food was out of the question for her tonight. Her churning stomach would never tolerate it. Seconds later found Mary Kate, alone and miserable, lying across that bed built for lovers.

"What am I going to do?" she moaned aloud, turning over to stare at the ceiling. She thought of her mother, of the choices that parent had once made, and wondered if she'd gone through the same agony of indecision before giving up her dreams and opting for marriage. Probably she had, Mary Kate realized. And how did her mother feel about those choices today? Did she have the secret regrets Mary Kate had always suspected she had? Or was she really as happy as she seemed to be? Suddenly Mary Kate had to know for sure.

She sat up and glanced at her watch, noting it was just after seven. That meant it was midnight in Ireland—not really too late for a woman as desperate as she was to call for help. Mary Kate pulled open the drawer of the nightstand to extract a list of phone numbers, one of which belonged to her grandmother, and then began to dial. She needed to hear her mother's voice, and she needed to hear it now. Thanks to the miracle of the telephone, she could.

A short time later the call went through. The connection wasn't a wonderful one, but Mary Kate warmed all over when she heard her mother say "Katy? Is something wrong?"

"Yes," Mary Kate blurted. "I mean no." She swallowed nervously. "I, uh, just wanted to ask you something."

Her mother laughed across the miles. "It must be something terribly important."

"It is." She swallowed again. "Are you happy?"

Dead silence followed her question. Then her mother said, "Yes I am. I love Ireland."

Mary Kate sighed. "I don't mean that. I want to know if you're happy with your life. Do you have regrets about getting married so young and never getting to be an interior decorator?"

There was another long silence and then a quiet "Before I answer, let me ask you a question."

"Okay."

"Are *you* happy?"

Mary Kate nearly strangled on the huge lump that immediately formed in her throat. "I've never been so miserable in my whole life."

"Want to talk about it?"

She certainly did. Mary Kate spilled her sad tale for the next several minutes, sprinkling it liberally with tears. Her mother remained silent until she had finished, when she murmured, "What a lucky young woman you are."

"Lucky?"

"Lucky. You've got it all, Katy—a man willing to give you his future, a house you two can grow into, and a shop where you can hide when you feel smothered. What more could you possibly want?"

Mary Kate smiled through her tears. "Put that way, I can't think of a thing."

"Times have certainly changed since I was your age. Wives didn't work unless they absolutely had to, and certainly not after they had children. Why, with your shop and Flynn's—it *was* Flynn, wasn't it?"

"Uh-huh."

"And Flynn's loan company right there in the house, you could even share baby-sitting duties once you started your family. What a setup!"

"But won't I be cheating my kids out of a normal childhood if I try to pursue a career while they're still young?"

"That depends on what you consider normal, I guess. Not long ago I read an article that said over fifty percent of all mothers with children ages six years and under are in the work force. The figure was quite a bit higher for children ages seven to sixteen. That tells me 'normal' isn't what it used to be."

"Wow," Mary Kate murmured, thinking of some of the working mothers she'd met since she opened her shop. Obviously happy juggling their families and careers, they talked about laundry detergents and the latest marketing trends in

the same breath. Surely she could do the same. But woul'
she look back someday and have regrets? She still didn'
know. "You never answered my question."

"I didn't, did I?" her mother replied, adding. "Well, yo'
can rest easy, Katy. I'm happy with the choices I made. Oh
I look at you every once in a while and wonder if *I* could'v'
succeeded in the business world, but I don't have regret'
Besides, my life isn't over yet. There's still time to tr'
something new, especially now that my last chick has flow'
the coop."

Mary Kate laughed. "Thanks, Mom. I love you."

"I love you, too. And I want you to promise me som'
thing."

"What's that?"

"I want you to wait until your dad and I get back in th'
States before you two tie the knot."

"Assuming we *do* tie the knot," Mary Kate responde'
"He may never want to see me again."

Soft laughter greeted that worry. "He's Irish, isn't he?'

"Yes."

"With a fair share of stubborn?"

"More than fair."

"There'll be a wedding."

Still laughing, Mary Kate hung up the phone a momer'
later. She lay back on the bed, rubbing her eyes, which stun'
from too many tears, and thinking of her mother's partin'
shot.

Would Flynn be back? Mary Kate remembered how she''
wounded his considerable ego by asking for more time. C'
would she have to go after him? She found the latter an in'
triguing idea and sat up, fully prepared to make that idea'
reality. Now that she finally understood she could hav'
everything, she wanted to get on with the rest of her life.

She got to her feet and moved to the bedroom door, fo'
the first time noticing that the room looked hazy. Creditin'

hat to her itchy eyes, she blinked to clear her vision. But it
didn't clear. Frowning, Mary Kate stepped into the hallway, only to discover the haze was even thicker there. She
sniffed, her heart lurching when she realized the haze was
actually smoke.

"Oh, my God!" she exclaimed, dashing down the stairs
leading to the kitchen. Halfway down, she had to stop and
rest her lungs, laboring in the acrid air. Waving her hands
in an attempt to clear it, she resumed her descent, arriving
in the kitchen seconds later, breathless and coughing. A
quick inspection of the smoke-filled room told her there was
no fire there.

Suddenly Mary Kate remembered her shop and the wood
stove she had, in her preoccupation, forgotten to douse that
night. Gasping her panic, she pivoted to race through the
ever-thickening haze to the door. She saw the licking flames
before she reached it and stopped short, screaming her terror.

"What if she won't come to the door?" Flynn asked
himself as he maneuvered the snowy streets of Denver,
heading back to Mary Kate. Barely an hour had passed since
he'd uttered what was intended to be a final goodbye—just
long enough to make him see that all his pride and fifty cents
might buy him a cup of coffee.

That realized, he'd finally confessed his need to be in
control, admitted it was high time to get a grip on it. He'd
vowed to backtrack and start over, taking things more
slowly, just as he'd planned to do in the first place. Mary
Kate had asked for time. Now all he had to do was convince her that he'd learned his lesson and would never again
ask her for more than she was willing to give—if he could
get her to listen to him . . . if he could get her to come to the
door.

Lost in the possible problems still facing him that night, Flynn barely registered the sound of a siren screaming behind him. He glanced in the rearview mirror, swerving automatically to the curb when he spotted a fast-approaching fire truck, red lights flashing. Shaking his head in sympathy for some poor soul, Flynn waited for the vehicle to pass him before he sped up again.

He saw the glow of those same red lights for several blocks before he turned down Mary Kate's street, then stomped on the gas pedal when he realized where the truck had stopped. Terror ran riot within him by the time he screeched to a halt, seconds later. He bounded from the Jeep, pushing through the gawking onlookers to frantically clutch the arm of the nearest fireman.

"Where's Mary Kate?" Flynn shouted over the commotion.

"Who?" asked the distracted man, never even looking up from the huge hose he was skillfully maneuvering.

"The woman who lives in the house."

That got the fire fighter's attention. He stopped and shook his head. "I don't know, man. We just got here."

Flynn abandoned him, frantically grabbing another of the scrambling firemen. "Did Mary Kate get out?" he demanded, his heart pounding with fear.

"She live here?"

"Yes."

"We'll find her. Anyone else inside?"

"No—maybe—I don't know," Flynn yelled out over his shoulder as he whirled to charge toward the house. The fireman lunged after Flynn, nearly tripping them both in his effort to stop his mad dash into the burning building.

"Wait!" the man cried. "Charlie's getting ready to go in now. He's trained. He'll find her." Flynn ignored him, twisting free, leaping onto the porch.

Mary Kate, safely sheltered in the shadows by concerned neighbors, screamed her terror when she spotted Flynn diving toward the open door. She broke free of the hovering women, shrieking his name.

He spun around at the sound of her voice, frantically scanning the maze of firemen and onlookers through the smoky darkness. Sobbing her anguish, Mary Kate burst from the crowd, stumbling to her knees in the trampled snow. Instantly at her side, Flynn hauled her up into a bone-crushing embrace. She clutched his arms to keep from falling again, burying her face in his sweater just over his thudding heart.

"Is anyone else in the house?" Flynn demanded, shaking her out of her daze. She shook her head. He yelled that information to the fireman who'd tried to save him earlier, and then dragged Mary Kate through the parting crowd to safety.

"I'm so sorry," she cried when they reached the yard's edge. "So sorry."

Flynn held her even tighter. "Shh," he soothed. "Everything's going to be all right now."

"How can you say that?" she wailed, breaking free. "Your house is in flames and it's all my fault."

"What are you talking about?" he demanded.

"I forgot to douse the stove. This whole thing is *my* fault—"

"Do you think I care what happens to that house?" he exploded.

"But all that money you've spent on it, all that work—"

"Forget the money. Forget the work. Forget the house, dammit. You're alive. That's all that matters." Flynn's strong arms engulfed her once more, and his searing kiss branded her as his forever.

* * *

What seemed like an eternity passed before the fire truck drove off into the night and the last curious onlooker wandered away. Arm in arm, Flynn and Mary Kate climbed the steps of the porch and entered the building. Since the fire had wreaked havoc on the electrical wiring in the shop, they used the beam of the flashlight Flynn had retrieved from the Jeep to assess the damage there.

The shop lay in ruins, a charred jumble of what used to be shelves, counters and merchandise. Smoky air stung their eyes, and the reek of the smoldering debris was so thick they could taste it. In the corner of the room stood the stove, its door still gaping—a sight that reduced Mary Kate to bitter tears. With difficulty, Flynn coaxed her back into the hallway, which was now slippery with mud and soot. Carefully avoiding the sodden mess, they then ascended the stairs together.

Thankful that the electricity on the second and third floors was wired to a breaker that hadn't been affected by the blaze, Flynn and Mary Kate made a quick inspection of the upper portion of the house. Due to the quick response of the fire department to Mary Kate's call, the area had sustained only minor water and smoke damage. The atmosphere was just as acrid there, though, and Mary Kate doubted that the smell of the fire would ever leave the house.

"Oh, why didn't I just let you get that darned central heating?" she moaned when they finished their tour and walked into her bedroom to get her valuables. She plopped down on her unscathed bed and lay back, covering her eyes. Flynn stretched out beside her with his legs sprawled over the edge, and pulled her hands away from her face.

"You've got to put it behind you," he said for the hundredth time, propping his elbow on the bed and leaning over to kiss her.

"How can I?" she asked, rolling over on her side to face him. "Everything's ruined."

"Only temporarily," he told her. "We'll start cleanup tomorrow. In no time you'll be back in business again." He reached out then, taking her in his arms. "Thank God you're okay. I nearly died when I saw where that fire truck had stopped."

"You didn't know about the fire before you got here?" Mary Kate asked, frowning into the front of his sweater.

"No."

Confused, she eased free and sat up on the bed. "Then why did you come back?"

Flynn sat up, too, and gave her a sheepish grin. "To apologize for being such an idiot earlier tonight. I didn't mean to press you, you know. I'd planned to take my time, ease into a proposal after we'd lived together for a while." He laughed uneasily. "I should've known I'd never be able to do it. I don't have that kind of patience...." His sentence faded into a lusty sigh. "I know I'm bossy, but if you'll just stick around for a while, I swear you're going to see a changed man."

"Oh, Flynn," she cried, throwing her arms around him. "I don't want a changed man, just one willing to compromise every once in a while."

"You've got it," he hastily assured her. "Smooth sailing from now on, and just to show you how sincere I am, the next marriage proposal is yours—even if I have to wait the rest of my life to hear it."

"Speaking of proposals," Mary Kate said, once more easing out of his embrace to drop to her knees on the floor directly in front of him, arms crossed over his denim-clad thighs. "Will you marry me?"

Flynn sat in stunned silence for a split second and then came to life, pulling her off the floor and full on top of him as he fell back on the bed. A twist and roll reversed their positions, and Mary Kate found herself flat on her back, with her hands pinned over her head.

"Do you mean it?" he demanded hoarsely.

"I mean it."

"No doubts?"

"No doubts."

"Hot damn!" he exclaimed, smothering her lips with an urgency that left no doubt as to his reply. Several fevered kisses later, he dragged himself off her. "How do you feel about a midnight wedding?"

"Can't do it," Mary Kate regretfully replied. "I promised my mom we'd wait until she and Dad got back home."

"You told your mom we were getting married?"

"No," Mary Kate said with a laugh. "*She* told *me*. Apparently she knows her Irishmen well."

"What *are* you talking about?" Flynn demanded, clearly baffled.

"I'll explain later," she promised. "Right now you've got to board up the windows in the shop so no one will come inside and steal my things tonight."

"Good point," Flynn agreed, getting slowly to his feet. "I'd hate for some looter to get this bed. I planned on us making our first baby here."

"Oh, you did, huh?"

"Yeah," he said, quickly adding, "No rush, of course."

"Of course," she agreed dryly, joining him. Together they packed what she would need that night and then began to descend the steps.

"You know, honey," Flynn said, breaking off to ask, "It *is* all right to call you 'honey,' isn't it?"

Biting her lip to keep from laughing at his uncharacteristic attempt at keeping the peace, she nodded.

"You know, *honey*," he then continued, "when we redo the shop, I'd like to change the layout just a little."

"How?" she asked, frowning.

"Well, I never really liked the arrangement of the shelves. If we turned them in the other direction, you'd get more aisle space."

"If we turned them in the other direction, I'd get ripped off," Mary Kate countered.

"You wouldn't!" Flynn exclaimed. "We could get one of those concave mirrors and mount it on the ceiling so—"

"I'm *not* having one of those things on my ceiling!" she retorted.

"But—"

"No!"

They stopped on the steps, glaring at each other, ready to do battle. Then they both burst into laughter.

"So much for compromise," Flynn muttered.

"And smooth sailing," she added.

"Yeah." He heaved a sigh. "This marriage business may be tougher than I thought. Do you think we've got what it takes to survive together?"

"*Exactly* what it takes," she assured him with a tender smile. "Love...and the luck of the Irish."

* * * * *

Silhouette Special Edition

presents

★ LOVE AND GLORY ★

from
Lindsay McKenna

Introducing a gripping new series celebrating our men—and women—in uniform. Meet the Trayherns, a military family as proud and colorful as the American flag, a family fighting the shadow of dishonor, a family determined to triumph—with **LOVE AND GLORY!**

June: A QUESTION OF HONOR (SE #529) leads the fast-paced excitement. When Coast Guard officer Noah Trayhern offers Kit Anderson a safe house, he unwittingly endangers his own guarded emotions.

July: NO SURRENDER (SE #535) Navy pilot Alyssa Trayhern's assignment with arrogant jet jockey Clay Cantrell threatens her career—and her heart—with a crash landing!

August: RETURN OF A HERO (SE #541) Strike up the band to welcome home a man whose top-secret reappearance will make headline news . . . with a delicate, daring woman by his side.

Silhouette Romance®

LONG, TALL TEXANS

Diana Palmer brings you the second Award of Excellence title
SUTTON'S WAY

In Diana Palmer's bestselling Long, Tall Texans trilogy, you had a mesmerizing glimpse of Quinn Sutton—a mean, lean Wyoming wildcat of a man, with a disposition to match.

Now, in September, Quinn's back with a story of his own. Set in the Wyoming wilderness, he learns a few things about women from snowbound beauty Amanda Callaway—and a lot more about love.

He's a Texan at heart . . . who soon has a Wyoming wedding in mind!

The Award of Excellence is given to one specially selected title per month. Spend September discovering *Sutton's Way* #670 . . . only in Silhouette Romance.

RS670-1R

Silhouette Romance®

JOIN TOP-SELLING AUTHOR
EMILIE RICHARDS
FOR A SPECIAL ANNIVERSARY

Only in September, and only in Silhouette Romance, we are bringing you Emilie's twentieth Silhouette novel, *Island Glory* (SR #675).

Island Glory brings back Glory Kalia, who made her first—and very memorable—appearance in *Aloha Always* (SR #520). Now she's here with a story—and a hero—of her own. Thrill to warm tropical nights with Glory and Jared Farrell, a man who doesn't want to give any woman his heart but quickly learns that, with Glory, he has no choice.

Join Silhouette Romance for September and experience a taste of *Island Glory*.

RS675-1